Praise for CB Samet

I0542869

Four-time award winning

GRAY HORIZON: 2019 Readers' Favorite Bronze Winner in Thriller category

MASTERS FILE: 2018 Readers' Favorite Honorable Mention in Romantic Suspense category

"Samet's prose vacillates skillfully between various registers, expressing sensuality, suspense, and humor, as needed."

— KIRKUS REVIEW (ON ROMANCING THE SPIRIT SERIES BOOKS 1-6)

"CB Samet is a master of the craft."

— READERS' FAVORITE REVIEWER (ON WHYTE KNIGHT)

Phoenix's Phantom

A ROMANCING THE SPIRIT NOVELLA

CB SAMET

Romancing the Spirit

A ROMANCING THE
SPIRIT NOVELLA

PHOENIX'S PHANTOM

CB SAMET

One

Phoenix crept down the gray stone staircase, using the flashlight on her mobile phone to light the way. The cavernous underground room spread out before her. Without the beam from her phone, she would have been in total darkness, yet, she still would have known her way around. She'd wandered beneath the theater so many times, her feet knew the number of steps descending into the circular chamber.

Each time she came here, she marveled at the mosaic pattern of light and dark blue stones on the floor, large gray columns, and overhanging archway. But what drew her here time and again wasn't the solitude and isolation of the room; it was the music she heard within it—breathtaking and beautiful music sung by a ghost haunting this chamber.

She'd found the large room while following the sound of a baritone from her backstage changing room one day. The voice had led her down the hallway to a storage closet where she'd discovered a hidden door, behind which a set of stairs plunged into blackness.

Now, standing once again in the large chamber and surrounded in chilled air and the smell of old stone, she began singing *Come What May* from the musical *Moulin Rouge*. She didn't have the voice projection or classical training required for opera, but that suited her perfectly since she preferred the exchange of dialogue and song in musicals.

The acoustics of the room took her version of the melody and reverberated the sound off the walls, echoing the tune into something both eerie and beautiful. She'd learned she could sing almost any Broadway tune in order to summon the spirit lingering down here, if the ghostly voice hadn't already initiated the singing prior to her arrival.

Before she reached the second verse, she heard his voice, warm and mesmerizing as liquid gold. Awe filled her as his voice enveloped her. Their voices entwined seamlessly, and she imagined a soft guitar playing in the background.

She didn't know the phantom's name. They had no interaction beyond singing. She didn't even know what he looked like or how old he'd been when he died. Not knowing his name, she had given him one—Gaston.

Phoenix had known the gift of seeing or hearing ghosts would manifest at some point in her life since her father and sister had the gift, and she was pleasantly surprised to be visited by a singing ghost, if a little distraught after discovering that he only ever sang.

When their duet concluded, she stayed quiet for a moment, letting Gaston pick the next song. He began to serenade her with *Some Enchanted Evening*. Even though the *South Pacific* song was a male solo, she joined him.

This time, something felt different. His voice grew louder and edgier, overpowering hers. She stopped singing and listened. Something in the urgency of his tone and the caution in his voice conveyed danger. Unlike the many other occasions she'd come down here and enjoyed fun or peaceful duets, this time she sensed he was warning her about something.

What hazards could possibly lay ahead of her? She sang musicals at a theater in New York City. Fear of an injury benching her always lingered in the back of her mind, but she didn't do anything hazardous outside of the workplace. Her only other fear was laryngitis. Perhaps he was cautioning her to stay away from him, but that made no sense; he was a singing ghost. What was more harmless than him?

"I don't know what you're trying to tell me," she said with frustration into the empty room when Gaston finished the song. "If you can sing, you can speak. Tell me who you are. Tell me why you're here."

She'd asked him a dozen times before for more information, but since he'd never given her an answer in the past, she didn't expect one this time. Disappointed in the ghost's continued lack of response, she turned and climbed the stairs back to the closet near the backstage offices of the theater.

LANCE PACKED several bags of luggage in the loft bedroom where he'd spent the last week on vacation. He relocated several times a year for his work in the entertainment business, but this time he was excited to return to New York for a more permanent position.

Behind him, the creak of footsteps coming up the stairs to his room caught his attention. His door slowly swung open.

"Hello, Nana." Even without looking, he knew she approached by the slow footsteps.

"You're off again," she said wistfully.

Although he'd already told her he had a new job in the US, he explained again, "It's a theater in New York. They need a new stage director."

She leaned against the doorframe, her lined face carrying a soft smile. "You were happier when you were the one on stage." She crossed her arms. "And the more time you spend in America, the more you start to sound like a North American."

He turned to look at her. "I'm happy. I enjoyed the stage, but I found I have stronger talents elsewhere. Who was it that said 'follow your talents not your dreams?' Besides, I'm rewarded every time one of the young talents I mentor succeeds."

"I wish you didn't have to go for such long stretches. I'm an old woman, you know. My days are numbered."

He walked over and kissed her cheeks, first one side and then the other. "Everyone's days are numbered, Nana. And you've been using that line for the better part of two decades." Still, he would miss her and wasn't sure when his next holiday would bring him back to her. He squeezed her arm.

Her warm smile faltered, her spine going rigid.

He pulled back. "What's wrong?"

"You do need to go." Her gaze turned distant. "She needs you."

Lance swallowed hard. He didn't like that look in his grandmother's eyes, but he knew it all too well. As long as he'd known her, she'd had an uncanny ability to predict the future. A rough outline and nothing precise, but often right regardless. Everyone in the family knew to heed her warnings. She'd once explained that spirits spoke to her, telling her of luck and danger. While Lance found this an insufficient explanation, he knew enough to pay attention when she had one of her premonitions.

"Who needs me, Nana?" he asked gently.

The one whose song you never finished. She's always needed you. But this time there's danger."

"What danger?" The hairs on his arms rose.

"You'll know. Keep on your toes." She blinked away the distant gaze before patting his cheek as though she hadn't just told him something terrible was on the horizon.

Lance thought about his grandmother's many predictions—when Tommy fell off his roof and broke his arm; when Aunt Georgia wore high heels to Mave's wedding and twisted her ankle.

But they weren't always accurate. When he'd left for a performance position in New York years ago, Nana had told him the spirits ordained he would find his match, the woman he would spend his life sharing dreams and happiness with. That hadn't happened. Or maybe it could have, but fate had stolen the opportunity.

Nothing could be done about those events now, though he'd never stopped fantasizing about what might have been under different circumstances.

He zipped up his bags and turned back to his grandmother. "Video chat once a week. Okay?"

"You're going to do great. Go break a leg." She winked at him.

~

"PULL YOURSELF TOGETHER, HARRY." Bowman sat beside the fidgeting old man on a bench in Central Park.

With trembling hands, Harry dabbed a handkerchief to his moist brow despite the cool fall breeze. "This wasn't supposed to happen."

"Accidents happen," Bowman tried to reassure him.

If the man didn't calm down, he would give himself a stroke or heart attack right here on the lawn. Bowman wasn't about to lock lips and perform CPR on anyone, even if Harry was willing to sell the theater to him.

But Harry didn't own the old building yet; his brother did.

"It wasn't an accident," Harry countered, his voice thick with misery. His gaze darted around as if he was afraid the two of them were being watched. "I killed a man. I meant to poison Cillian—something I at least thought would be an act of mercy given his state of health—but the wrong man ate the medication."

"A tragic accident," Bowman insisted in as gentle a tone as he could, but honestly, how much longer would he have to listen to Harry's self-flagellation and blathering?

"You could turn yourself in," Bowman suggested, as if Harry had simply failed to parallel park correctly instead of poisoned the wrong person.

No one suspected wrongful death in the man Harry was referring to, but if Harry turned himself in, the scandal might disrupt Cillian's life enough he would be willing to sell the theater. Bowman doubted he would get so lucky.

Harry shook his head violently as he stared, hunched over, at the ground. "I'd die in jail. I'm done. I can't conspire like this anymore."

Bowman scowled at the implication that some fault lay with him. He'd never told Harry to kill his own brother; he'd merely discussed how the money Harry would make from the sale of Cillian's building would take care of his debts and unburden his children. If Harry chose to take action, Bowman couldn't be held responsible, even if he'd planted the seed and reaped the benefit.

Sure, Bowman manipulated people's thoughts, but their actions were still subject to free will. The responsibility and consequences lay solely with the physical perpetrator.

He shifted his gaze across the park to Sheep Meadow where people threw balls or lounged on towels, soaking up the early autumn rays. His lips thinned in disdain. He was a man of ambition and achievement, not a sheep lazily grazing on wasted leisure time.

Bowman needed the deed in Harry's possession since his stodgy older brother refused to sell the run-down theater as he clung to some philanthropic desire to preserve the arts. Unlike his brother, Harry saw reason and was willing to sell—even though he was a basket case at this particular moment. And apparently capable of murder.

A heavy finality settled in Harry's tone as he pushed up from the bench with his cane. "I won't be a part of this anymore." In slow, frail steps, he ambled away down the walking path.

Bowman didn't follow. If he'd thought to record the conversation, a murder charge on Cillian's brother might be damaging enough to ruin him—except that it might also earn him public sympathy and help him.

Bowman couldn't enlist Harry's help if he was going to fall apart at the first stumbling block. However, Harry would still be willing to sell the theater to Bowman if Cillian was forced to surrender it. For this reason, Bowman needed to maintain a cordial relationship with Harry.

As for nudging the theater out of Cillian's grasp, Bowman would need to get more creative. New York didn't need to cling to another floundering theater, and the high-rise condominium he could put there would be infinitely more profitable and fulfill a societal need for residential space.

Bowman needed eyes and ears inside the theater to help him create the right opportunity. If he couldn't financially undermine the owner through the brother, perhaps some other tragedy could hasten the timeline to foreclosure. Part of the key to Bowman's success was always having a back-up plan.

Two

Phoenix was soaking her feet in Epsom salt when her sister called. She set the phone to speaker mode and leaned back on the couch, tilting her head to look at the ceiling of her cozy loft apartment.

"Hi, Jenny."

"I'm shocked and amazed you answered your phone. You finally have a day off?"

"It's showbiz. Showbiz never stops."

They were currently rehearsing ten a.m. to six p.m. six days a week. When the show went live in four weeks, the performers would do eight shows a week—two on Wednesdays and Saturdays, off on Mondays. Phoenix's job was a dream come true, dancing on stage and living in New York. Some days her love for the stage hardly made performing seem like work, and other days her exhausted body reminded her just how taxing it really was. Yet, when an audience of strangers applauded—and even stood—showering the cast with adoration, there were no words to describe the soaring elation she felt.

"How is *West Side Story* coming?"

"Good. It's especially awesome that I have a lead role, although my feet currently disagree with my opinion." Phoenix swirled her feet in the soothing water.

"*West Side Story*, though? Isn't it kind of old?" Jenny asked.

"It was first performed in 1957, but any version of *Romeo and Juliet* is never too old for the stage."

"You're a hopeless romantic," Jenny said.

"Says the woman who's found her match," Phoenix countered. Her sister was in a serious relationship with a fellow lawyer.

"Still seeing ghosts?" Jenny asked.

"Hearing, not seeing. You?"

"Thankfully not since the last one moved on."

The sisters had inherited their father's supernatural gift of seeing and/or hearing ghosts. The last one Jenny had interacted with helped solve her own murder before moving on from haunting the living world.

"I gave my ghost a name," Phoenix said. "He won't talk to me, only sings. And he won't tell me his name."

"Oh."

"Gaston. In honor of Gaston Leroux."

"Um...?"

"He wrote *The Phantom of the Opera* original novel," Phoenix explained.

"What was the phantom's name in the opera? Why not call your ghost that?"

"The phantom's name was Erik, but Erik was an actual flesh and blood man, so I wanted a different name. My ghost does have a tragic sort of vibe, but he's friendly."

"So, why not Casper?"

"It's Gaston. Get behind it."

Jenny chuckled. "Okay. Okay. Gaston the ghost. Actually, that has a nice ring to it."

Phoenix took her feet out of the basin and began toweling them off.

"How is the historical claim coming?" Jenny asked.

"I filled out the request for evaluation and sent it to the Landmark Preservation Commission."

"Supporting documents?"

"I've gathered all of the reports, maps, and articles I could find." Phoenix had done the tedious work of data collecting, and the effort would pay off if the theater became a historic landmark. She loved the building and wanted it to have the safety of preservation since the owner wasn't in good health. And she wanted to give this gift to Gaston. His history dwelled in The Magnolia, even if Phoenix didn't know his story.

"Do you think you've made a strong case?"

"I think so. And I have a preservation group willing to speak on the building's behalf if and when we get a designated hearing," Phoenix said.

"I have faith. You'll get your hearing."

"If I gave them one look at the list of needed repairs, the Landmark Preservation Committee would see just how historic The Magnolia really is."

Jenny chuckled. "Maybe once you get that historical designation some societies will work to help restore it."

"I bet it would look magnificent restored."

〜

PHOENIX SAT in the third row of the theater with her co-performers surrounding her. The seats were plush red, if a little worn with age, and the old wooden frames were sturdy but creaked with movement, though certainly not loud enough to disrupt an on-stage performance. She loved the antique ambience of the theater, how all of the wood molding was ornately carved and the balcony seating arched in baroque style. The place felt like a second home—a luxurious one she didn't have to pay rent on.

Some of the other performers sat with legs crossed, others slouched, and a few had their feet propped up on the seat in front of them. They spent so much time together, they felt like a family—the kind you adored, quirks and all, but were glad you didn't actually live with. From her experience, tight bonds were formed in the theater world.

Carrie starred in *West Side Story* as Anita, the feisty, assertive friend of Maria's, which rather fit her real-life relationship with Phoenix.

Dom played Bernardo, Maria's brother and Anita's boyfriend, and leader of The Sharks. He was a broad chested man who'd lamented having to shave his beard for the part.

Whit played Chino, an angry, murderous Shark, who was actually a super sweet man outside of his role despite a penchant for continually practicing making a menacing expression throughout the day, on and off stage, for his role.

Ray starred as Tony, the love-stricken former leader of The Jets who fell in love with Maria. Ray was another nice guy, though in real life he was in love with the actor playing Pepe.

Lee played Riff, the quick-tempered Jet leader

murdered by Bernardo. He had a strong voice and quick feet.

Silas, a scrawny kid of twenty-two, aptly played Baby John. He was an easy-going people pleaser, and Phoenix suspected he was working two jobs to make ends meet.

All of these coworkers along with a dozen or so more had gathered in front of the stage for an announcement. The context of the announcement presented no surprise. Their director, Arif, had been a large, sweaty man with a warm smile who'd died young, though not surprisingly, from a heart attack. It was only a matter of time before they announced his replacement. The part they anxiously awaited to hear was who the new director would be.

Everyone's eyes were fixed on the stage and backdrop of thick, red-ribboned curtains. Unlike during a show, the house lights were all on, illuminating the theater so the performers could see each other and the stage and anyone on stage could see those in the seats.

A man walked on stage wearing a gray three-piece suit with a silver sheen over a crisp white shirt. Tidy yet voluminous brown hair framed a handsome face with a strong jawline covered by a short beard, slightly more than stubble but neatly trimmed. He had a narrow nose, dark eyes, and ...

Phoenix's heart revved at the sight of him. She sat in stunned, silent disbelief as the man from her past stood in front of them and introduced himself.

After Lance Hamilton had left, she'd never thought she would see him again. She'd heard he'd worked his way up to becoming a stage director and thought the role suited his charismatic personality, but she hadn't expected him to become *her* stage director. The theater grew uncomfortably warm as her chest tightened. A rush of emotions jumbled and twisted through her like a kaleidoscope.

Seeing Lance was like seeing a ghost from her past, but unlike the musical voice in the chamber below the theater who lifted her spirits, the idea of working with the man to whom she compared all other men invoked a sense of dread.

Lance spoke to the gathered members of the cast with calm reassurance, promising the show would go on despite the loss everyone had suffered when Arif died. As he talked, he removed his suit jacket and slung it over one shoulder, casually walking the length of the stage back and forth while making eye contact with everyone.

Phoenix's thoughts raced. Had he known before he even accepted the job that she worked here? Wouldn't he have seen her name on the list of actors and actresses? Had he chosen this job knowing she performed here? Did he want to work with her?

No. He was here to do a job, and she knew it had nothing to do with her. She'd never even told him about her crush on him eight years ago.

Eight year since they missed a connection that might have been. Had it been so long? Surely, he was married by now, probably even had kids.

She tried to gauge how professional she could be working with him when just the sight of him on stage churned an old longing she thought had died.

Their professional interactions had to work. She loved New York and loved her job. A silly, old crush wouldn't interfere with the life she'd built here.

She thought of the musical voice beneath The Magnolia. She always had Gaston to distract her, carry her to a distant magical realm of exquisite beauty and splendor when reality was too hard. She had the phantom and her other love—this theater, with a hundred years of history brimming with heart and soul. These intangibles brought her happiness and would keep her from pining for a man she hardly knew any more.

With Gaston, she felt understood. With Lance, she felt ... exposed.

Setting her jaw, Phoenix crossed her arms and found her resolve. She could keep her interactions with Lance professional, and this time around would be easier because they wouldn't be performing together. Still, she couldn't help but wonder if he was currently in a relationship.

BOWMAN SLIPPED a napkin in his lap and waited for the scrawny, nervous kid to follow his lead. Silas did so, scanning the room at Serafina's as he salivated at the sight of fine Italian cuisine heaped on plates at adjacent tables.

Ugh, starving artists. Bowman suppressed an eye roll. Yet, he was counting on the young actor's poverty being the key to his cooperation.

After approving the wine and watching the glasses poured, Bowman made small talk, biding his time and feigning interest in the kid until the alcohol and ambience morphed Silas into a malleable putty of susceptibility.

The twenty-something droned on about his role as Baby Face in the musical. As animated as the boy was, one would think he was in the process of curing cancer rather than playing a minor character in *West Side Story*.

"In a few years, maybe I'll be cast as Riff."

Bowman neither knew nor cared which character Silas referred to. "Fascinating. Well, you must have studied hard in school."

Silas gulped down half of his second glass of wine. "Yup. Two years at Columbia."

"Quite an accomplishment." Not even a full four, Bowman noted.

"Yeah."

"Quite expensive, too."

"Yeah, that too."

"It's hardly fair to an aspiring talent such as yourself—all that debt when you have to live in The Big Apple, a metropolis with such a high cost of living."

"It sucks, man. Living off Ramen noodles, renting a dump apartment with paper-thin walls, and hoping not to get mugged on the way home. But it'll get better as I get better parts in bigger productions. Theater is a dream come true. I'm an *actor*. How cool is that?"

When the food arrived, Silas began shoveling it into his mouth. Bowman estimated his level of refinement was about one rung on the ladder above dropping his head to his plate and eating like a dog.

Bowman didn't move to pick up his silverware. He decided he'd wait until he dismissed Silas, and then he could enjoy his cannelloni alone.

"Have you considered working two jobs? Making money on the side?" Bowman asked.

"I tried that, but there aren't enough hours in a day,"

Silas said around a mouth full of chicken parmigiana. "We're always refurbishing or prepping costumes or patching up props when we're not rehearsing."

"What if your second job paralleled your current job, and the only time commitment was a meal at a nice restaurant?"

Silas swallowed a bite of garlic bread. "What do you mean?"

"I have financial interests in the theater. There's a new director now, and I want to make sure everything runs smoothly. I would like weekly updates on the inner workings of the staff."

Silas blinked at him. "I thought Cillian Byrne owned the theater."

"Oh, he does. I own nothing. But I still have financial interests. I need eyes and ears on the inside to learn the work flow." He needed to save this part of the city from the same decay of the rotting relic of a theater.

Bowman gauged Silas's interest. He'd done a thorough check on each of the performers, looking for the weakest link. Who needed money. Who had little family nearby. Who could be manipulated into doing his bidding. Silas had been the obvious choice.

"You want me to spy for you?" Silas asked, glancing around the room in the first hint of reservation he'd displayed since taking a seat and being distracted by food.

Maybe some higher life form did inhabit the kid's brain, Bowman thought.

"In a good way," he assured the budding actor. "In the interest of all." He unlocked his mobile phone, entered a number on the calculator app, and slid it over to Silas.

The kid looked at the phone with wide eyes and gulped. "This is your offer?"

"Every week. Just for information. Just for my peace of mind. Nothing intrusive. Nothing dangerous."

"And we have meals like this together?"

"Yes."

"I'm your spy." Silas smiled, though completely devoid of any deviousness those three little words implied.

"Inside man," Bowman corrected.

"I'm your inside man."

Three

Lance sat in a portable nylon chair under a perfect September afternoon sun. He wore jeans and a T-shirt, soaking up the seventy-degree weather. The days would soon grow shorter and colder, but by then the show would move from rehearsals to live and he would be too busy to think about the weather.

In front of him, middle-school-aged girls pounded a ball down the field.

"It's good to have you back in town," Yoshi said.

Lance clinked his soda bottle to his friend's. "I've missed New York. And your little ones have grown up."

Somewhere in the blur of cleats, tall socks, and pony-tails were Yoshi's twin girls.

"It's been something else watching them grow," Yoshi said with endearment. "Any little Hamiltons in the making?"

"Ah, no, mate." The idea of a family appealed, but many steps stood between him and that sort of undertaking.

"Still searching for *the one*?"

Lance had been surrounded by beautiful women his entire professional life—young, lean, slender as tulips, and full of talent. And he had to have them all, a touch and a taste as he tried and failed to recreate the chemistry he'd felt with Phoenix Wiley. He winced to think of how many first dates he'd spent silently measuring women against a memory.

"I couldn't find that spark, Yoshi." Lance had tried to accept defeat. He'd cut back on his dating once he realized his infatuation with a relationship that had never happened was unfair to the other women he'd pursued.

And yet ...

"You sound like you've given up," Yoshi said.

"I took a break. I asked myself what I really had to offer a woman. What did a long-term relationship with Lance Hamilton look like? My career in show business had been tenuous at best, and I'd no savings, nothing for a family."

Yoshi blinked at him. "How long a break did you take?"

"Two years. Two years of working hard, proving I could be the best director I could be, and starting a nest egg."

"So, break's over?" Yoshi took a long gulp of soda as he watched one of his daughters score a goal. "Yeah! Go, Minny!"

"I found Phoenix."

Beautiful Phoenix Wiley—whose passion and fire lived up to her mythical namesake. The passing years had brought to her a maturity without stealing her youthful exuberance. She was slender with just the right amount of curve in her thighs and hips. Her oval face held high cheekbones that weren't too prominent. And when she smiled ...

"Oh, yeah?" Yoshi grunted. "She still everything you remember? Sometimes those rose-colored glasses make the past seem grander than it was."

Lance shifted in his chair. "She had her whole career ahead of her as a talented dancer and singer when we met, and now she's a leading lady. She's still everything I remember. I just don't know how she feels about me." He thought about how she'd crossed her arms and practically glared at him when he'd introduced himself to the theater performers. "I remember sensing the chemistry eight years ago, but perhaps it was all one-sided. Rose-colored glasses and whatnot."

Lance had never forgotten Phoenix. Never could. They'd played minor characters together with one major scene: Liesl and Rolf dancing in the garden of the von Trapp estate singing *Sixteen Going on Seventeen* in *The Sound of Music.*

Phoenix hadn't been seventeen. She'd been twenty and four years younger than him. He'd looked forward to every performance with her—the singing, the long looks, the holding hands. When he'd learned she was dating someone, he subdued his emotions and never shared them with her. He wouldn't break up a relationship for his own desire to explore the chemistry he felt.

Then one day, she showed up puffy-eyed and morose. Lance had learned from other crew members that she'd broken up with her boyfriend. The problem was Lance had started dating a graphic designer in his apartment complex by then. He'd initiated the relationship because he refused to pine over a woman he couldn't have. But the designer was also incredibly sweet, and he didn't feel right dropping her just because Phoenix had become single.

He'd eventually drifted apart from the designer as their work schedule continually failed to align. At last, near the end of the run of *The Sound of Music*, Phoenix and he were backstage after their scene together.

"Will you go out with me?" he'd asked.

"Like a date?" Her hazel irises glowed like tiger's eyes in the soft light.

"Yes, a date."

"I'd like that." She smiled sweetly.

Those simple words had him floating on the clouds. He thought he could run through the hills of Switzerland singing about how alive they were with music. That night, they'd set a day and time.

Tragically, Phoenix's father's health declined unexpectedly, and she promptly left New York to return to North Carolina.

During her absence, Lance accepted another offer for a larger production. The step had simultaneously opened opportunities for him that led to becoming a stage director and wedged a gargantuan gap in his plans to court Phoenix. So, he'd let that flame extinguish, chalking up their separation to fate or destiny or whatever higher power seemed determined to interfere.

Now, the time and distance gap had closed, and he wanted to see if their proximity could spark something between them again.

"Coach! Penalty! Come on!" Yoshi jumped out of his seat, flapping his hands.

The outburst brought Lance back to the present and

back to the football game—er, soccer in this country. "She could be dating someone for all I know," he added glumly.

"Only one way to find out," Yoshi said, sitting back down.

"You're right. I need a spy." At Yoshi's dismayed look, Lance chuckled. "Kidding. I'll talk to her."

When he had the opportunity, he thought. So far, one week in and he hadn't had a chance to speak directly to her without a crowd of other cast members. He would have to find a way to create the opportunity.

PHOENIX TUGGED on her jazz shoes and played *As Long as You're Mine* from the *Wicked* soundtrack on her phone through a Blue Tooth speaker. She stood poised for a moment, alone on stage, letting the music wash over her. She felt the beat of the drums and piano. She loved to dance and loved her job. But most of all, she loved music.

Music was power. Music was magic. Music could bridge the gaps of gender, ethnicity, sexual orientation, and politics. It could reach into the depths of a person's soul and elevate their mood instantaneously. Music could trigger the amygdala and allow memories from decades ago to resurface.

She began to dance, stepping in time to the music and singing along with the lyrics. Swept away in the moment, she moved and swayed as if dancing on air.

A masculine figure stepped onto the stage, dressed in black slacks, black cape, and black mask. Phoenix was startled, but her steps never faltered, and she didn't stop dancing. The theater remained locked at night, so she knew it wasn't as though someone off the street had entered.

In fact, there was only one person it could be. One phantom. Her heart soared. He'd finally come.

She'd wondered if Gaston would ever reveal himself. He looked more solid than she'd thought he would, but she was no ghost expert. His body was lean and fit. Too bad the mask he wore covered his face entirely.

He started singing the male lyrics of the duet. His voice sounded different, but still beautiful; she wondered if the mask altered it or the open stage acoustics were different from the enclosed chamber beneath the theater.

He walked toward her, stepping in time to the music. Her heart lifted.

Would he dance with her? That would be a first.

Initially, they danced around each other without touching. But then they couldn't touch, could they?

Around and around they went, stepping and singing like a type of courtship. It felt magically surreal, intoxicatingly seductive, and a little dangerous.

When Gaston reached for her, she was surprised by the solidity of his touch. She knew little about spirits but expected them to be entirely incorporeal. Instead, his hands were warm and his touch felt exquisite as he led her through dance moves.

When the song stopped, his arms cradled her as he leaned over her while she arched backward. She could feel the beating of his heart, the heat of his breath, and the rise and fall of chest.

This was no ghost.

He was smiling, sweet and seductive, when he lifted the mask off his face.

Lance leaned closer for a kiss whispering her name, "Phoenix."

She gasped and pushed herself away from him. "Lance! What are you doing here?"

His face darkened with a mixture of rejection and confusion. "I thought we were having a rather beautiful moment."

She glanced around the stage. They were alone, and Gaston wasn't present. Her heart beat widely as her mind tried to make sense of the confusion of the situation. She thought she'd been dancing with her phantom, the being whose voice she had fallen in love with. Instead, she'd been dancing with the man of flesh and blood she'd fantasized about for years. She snatched her phone and grabbed her bag.

"You're leaving?" Lance asked.

Reality came crashing down on her fantasy, and she couldn't process it or even look at him. She'd ruined what might have been a romantic moment with Lance, but there was no fixing it. She couldn't explain that she'd mistaken him for a ghost—not without sounding unhinged.

Embarrassed and frustrated with herself, she managed to stammer, "I'm sorry. I have to leave."

LANCE STOOD ON THE STAGE, dumbfounded, and watched a flustered Phoenix rush away from him and out of the theater. He was baffled and a little infuriated by the entire situation as he began to regret letting her leave so abruptly. He hadn't had a chance to ask her to talk to him about what had upset her, other than the fact that she obviously hadn't been expecting to see him beneath the mask.

All week he'd been trying to catch her by herself so he could ask her if she had any interest in going on the date they'd never had.

Tonight, he'd been backstage, toying with costumes when he'd heard the music and followed the sound. Seeing Phoenix dancing alone, looking graceful and so incredibly gorgeous, had stolen his breath away. He'd slipped on the mask and cape in his hand and allowed himself to be drawn to her.

When she'd accepted him as a dance partner, his heart had stirred up the same delicious desire he'd once had for her. He didn't have to talk to her to gauge her interest and availability after all; they only needed to recreate the magic they'd once shared together on stage. Phoenix was majestically eloquent, such a mixture of fragility and strength.

For those short, mesmerizing minutes of music and dance, he'd dared to hope he could have the relationship fate had thwarted eight years ago.

Then, she'd shattered the beauty of the moment by her shock, or rather dismay, when he'd removed the mask and she'd seen his face. He'd charged in like a lovesick twenty-two-year-old instead of the director who should have asked her first.

Now, he paced the theater stage alone, frustration roiling through him like angry waves in a storm. Whom did she think she'd been dancing with? Was she seeing someone? No one in the production cast had Lance's build and voice, so how had she *not* known it was him? No one outside the theater would have access to the stage at this time of night.

He ran a hand through his hair, trying to beat back his anger. His behavior had been reckless. He needed to maintain a working relationship with his staff, and apparently, Phoenix wanted nothing to do with him. The way she'd darted off made that abundantly clear.

"MR. B, HOW'S IT ROLLING?" Silas beamed.

Bowman accepted the kid's weird handshake with its slide and snap as he tried to remember the last time anyone had showed this much enthusiasm when meeting with him.

Well, he was paying and feeding the kid. Still, he had full-time employees who barely managed to fake a smile when they saw him.

Apparently, he wasn't paying Silas enough for a decent hair cut though; he had wavy bangs hanging down in his eyes. Maybe the style was needed for his Baby Face role. He snapped the locks out of his eyes with a flick of his head as he tucked his hands in his baggy jeans.

They walked into the Chinese restaurant, and a server escorted them to a table. Silas ordered enough for three people, and Bowman ordered a lunch portion of vegetable lo mein. He'd initially regretted letting the young man choose the venue, but the inviting smell had Bowman interested in tasting the food. Besides, the plates cost a fraction of what he often had to pay to woo the people he was manipulating.

A strange twinge struck Bowman as Silas preemptively

thanked him for the upcoming meal. The sensation was so foreign to Bowman, he almost didn't recognize it.

Guilt.

He was using Silas for his own gain, but that was nothing new for Bowman. Perhaps the thought of destroying the kid's innocence had caused that twinge. But such was life. Someone would inevitably crush his spirit in this dog-eat-dog world. There would be other theaters where he could find some minor role to play after Bowman owned and demolished this one. Besides, Silas never needed to know how Bowman used the information he gleaned.

"How are rehearsals going?" Bowman asked. He didn't really care about rehearsals, but the question seemed like a good way to start the conversation about the theater, and he could then steer Silas in the appropriate direction.

"Going good. Our new director is pretty cool. Name's Lance Hamilton. Looks good too. Rocks this three-piece suit like Leonardo DiCaprio in *The Great Gatsby*."

Bowman arched an eyebrow as he squeezed lemon into his water.

"No? Simon Baker in *The Mentalist*?" Silas slurped his Coke. "How about Steve McQueen in *The Thomas Crown Affair*—1968 version?"

Bowman nodded, understanding the reference. "Good movie. He drove a 1968 Ferrari."

"Yeah, classy. Anyway, Lance is classy like that—the effortless kind. Maybe it's the British accent. Sometimes we joke and call him Sir Lancelot. He's good at coaching all the performers too. There's some tension between him and Phoenix—she's playing Maria—but Carrie says they like each other. There's some other dating on the set, like Whit and Rosa, so maybe Lance and Phoenix will hook up too. Seems risky, you know, with his position and all. But she's a looker—brunette with golden eyes. Good actress too. And nice. Can't blame him for wanting to cozy up with her."

The food arrived and Silas dove in, though it didn't stop him from talking. He described other relationship dynamics and who was jealous of whom for different roles they'd won.

Bowman rubbed his temple. He felt like he was suffering through one of his wife's soap operas, or worse; reality shows. Yet, Silas's enthusiasm and easy conversation took the edge off as Bowman tried to search for some useful morsel in the kid's information dump.

Somewhere in there was the key to the theater's demise.

Four

Phoenix called her sister Jenny as she sat on her yoga mat and stretched. She often spent her time before rehearsals with the same routine she followed before shows, stretching and hydrating.

Three days had passed since her impromptu dance with Lance. She'd wanted to discuss the issue with him, but they never had a moment alone. He was always surrounded by other cast members or staff who he was instructing. She was starting to wonder if that was by design. He had every right to avoid her after the way she'd rocketed off like Elphaba defying gravity in the musical *Wicked*.

"Hey, sis. How are you?"

"Good. I wanted to update you on the historical registry paperwork." Phoenix rambled for a few minutes about the topic, all the while thinking of Lance.

"What about your phantom?" Jenny asked.

"Still singing and not talking." Phoenix sighed as she leaned over to stretch her hamstring.

"I bet there's a story behind him. Something tragic.

Isn't the theater a hundred years old? Maybe there was a fire and he died, or jumped off the roof and committed suicide after some scandal."

"Morbid much? If I knew his real name, I could do a search." Phoenix extended her arms out as she balanced on one leg.

"Is there anybody you know in show biz who might know the building's history?"

Phoenix considered the question. "The owner perhaps. Cillian Byrne. He's emotionally attached to the theater, and I bet he's learned some things about it over the years. I'll talk to him this week."

"If it's a captivating story, the richer personal history might appeal to the Landmark Preservation Committee when it comes time to vote on making it a historical building. You could add it to your presentation."

"Good thinking." She arched to the left before blurting, "I danced with Lance."

"Lance? *The* Lance who you've been hung up on for years? Ooh. Do tell."

"He's our new stage director. I was shocked when he introduced himself to the group. I've been trying to wrap my head around my emotions, but it's hard when I see him every day." Her stomach did giddy flips whenever he addressed her to correct or improve a scene. "It seems so absurd to be this flustered over a guy I never actually dated and haven't seen in eight years."

"The heart wants what the heart wants," Jenny said wistfully.

"It still wants. I steal glimpses during rehearsal, hoping he doesn't notice."

"He's not seeing someone else this time?"

"No wedding ring, but I haven't outright asked him if he's dating someone."

"But he danced with you. Tell me it was more than just a rehearsal."

Phoenix straightened before pulling her leg behind her. "Not a rehearsal. I was dancing to *As Long as You're Mine* from the *Wicked* soundtrack, and he joined me on stage. It was just the two of us after hours. But he wore a mask, so I thought he was Gaston. I felt intoxicated, even spellbound, dancing and singing with him. Except, as we touched, I realized he was solid. When the song ended, he lifted the mask to kiss me."

Jenny let out a heartfelt sigh.

"And that's when I panicked, pushed him away, and ran out of the building."

"Are you serious?"

"Phoenix Wiley, moment-killer. It's sad to think the only male hands on my body for over a year have been for performances."

"No wonder, if running away is your response."

Phoenix groaned, reliving the humiliation.

Jenny snorted. "Talk to him."

"I will. I intend to. What if he's dating someone?"

What if he was mad at her for running away?

"Then he shouldn't have been dancing his way to a kiss with you."

"Yeah, you're right. But he looked so angry when I pushed him away. How do I explain my confusion? I can't tell him—*oh, I mistook you for a ghost I'm infatuated with who sings with me*."

33

"You got me there, but 'sorry' goes a long way. Apologize for freaking out, and see if he's receptive."

Phoenix frowned. She would need to practice the apology, rehearse such a performance a few times before she could speak with Lance and hope not to trip over her own tongue. She would confront him, but first she needed the right opportunity.

ON HER DAY OFF, Phoenix took a ride share to the Staten Island home of Cillian Byrne. His house was an expansive beauty of gray and white stone. The slate-colored gables were steep, creating a castle-like appearance. The home had a library, solarium, expansive kitchen, and six bedrooms. She'd first met with him here when they initially delved into the theater as a historical project.

Cillian's home health nurse greeted Phoenix with a smile and let her inside the house.

"Hi, Ann." She told herself she was here for paperwork. Truthfully, she wanted a story and a name for the man whose voice had become her favorite part of the day.

"Phoenix, you're looking too thin. You need to eat more between songs." Ann had a nest of disheveled red hair that somehow worked with her bright purple scrubs and perpetually warm smile.

"How is he?" Phoenix asked.

Ann shrugged as she led her through the house to the garden in the backyard. "Good days and bad days."

Phoenix had met Cillian when she'd been hired on at The Magnolia. He owned the theater, two nightclubs, and a restaurant in New York. His entertainment empire had once consisted of more, but he'd slowly partitioned off pieces to his grandchildren. Unfortunately, they hadn't had his work ethic, and one by one, the businesses fell into bankruptcy.

Whether seeing him was a reminder of their failure or if Cillian had intentionally alienated his family, Phoenix didn't know. She'd heard the last person he willed his fortune to was his brother rather than his offspring, but she sensed Harry Byrne didn't provide a source of much familial comfort or companionship either.

She had started visiting Cillian two years ago when she first presented the idea of making the theater a historical landmark. He'd been receptive to the idea, requiring that they meet regularly to discuss it. She suspected these mandatory meetings helped fill a loneliness in his life. The encounters served to fill a loneliness in hers too. Her parents had passed away, and her only sister lived down in Charlotte.

Cillian reminded her a little of her father, who'd been a judge. They both had a strong authoritarian presence when it came to business, yet a charismatic gentleness when it came to friendships. She was saddened to think Cillian's own children and grandchildren were missing out on knowing his greatness, but perhaps she only saw his softer side because she wasn't family. Perhaps he was a different person to them, holding them to higher expectations.

Cillian was walking the perimeter around his garden, wearing khaki pants and a blue cotton shirt as he toted a rolling oxygen tank behind him like a wheeled golf bag. The clear plastic tubing tethered him to the tank as it snaked around his ears to his nose.

She came up to walk beside him.

"Phoenix, aren't you looking lovely. How is the production coming along?"

"Arif's replacement is doing a great job. We're all on schedule for opening night."

"Arif," he said with sorrow in his voice. "You know he had lunch with me the very day he died. Such a tragedy."

Life is frail, Phoenix thought, briefly envisioning her parents. And yet beside her strolled a man in his mid-eighties who still persevered despite having emphysema and pulmonary fibrosis.

"How much do you know about the history of the theater?" Phoenix asked.

Cillian was a businessman and not a performer; he'd owned and operated a dozen establishments at one point and may not have had intimate knowledge about each of his proprietorships, but she wouldn't learn anything about her ghost if she didn't at least ask.

"Lots of history at that place," he answered.

"Anything in particular revolving around a male baritone? Maybe even something tragic?"

She'd tried to do her own online search, but without a name or even a general year to narrow her investigation down, she couldn't discover anything about the origin of the phantom who sang to her.

"Tragedy," he said in a distant, searching voice. "There was a story I once heard ... rumors, mind you. The year was 1923 and prohibition was in full force—never fully accepted in New York, but still a contentious topic.

Gaetano Reina was a budding crime boss of the Lucchese crime family, until his death in 1930 when Tommy Gagliano took over."

"The Gagliano crime family?" Phoenix had heard of them.

"Yes. Gaetano's legitimate operation was a monopoly on the ice box. His illegal activity was a smattering of everything—drugs, alcohol, weapons. The Magnolia was called the Theater of New Rotterdam at the time. It was said to have had an underground distillery with distribution tunnels to avoid the law."

Phoenix hung on his every word as she followed him to a bench where they both sat. She pictured the chamber the phantom had revealed to her, for the first time understanding what purpose it had probably served.

Cillian adjusted his oxygen tubing. "One of Gaetano's men operated that distillery. He took a fancy to a leading lady—Julia, I think her name was—but she was engaged to the lead actor, singer Charles, um, Goldberg, I believe. Anyway, Julia rejected Gaetano's man, who then sought to murder Charles in a fit of jealous rage. Protecting Charles, Julia stepped between the two feuding men and was shot dead. Gaetano's man fled the city. Charles tried to keep the show going, but the first performance he did without her, he died of a broken heart while singing on stage."

Phoenix blinked away tears, thinking of her ghost's lost love. She felt a little dizzy now, sitting after their slow promenade, perhaps it was the sad tale or exhaustion from many rehearsals.

She thought of Leroux's words from *The Phantom of the Opera*, "*Tonight I gave you my soul, and I am dead.*"

Gaston must have been Charles Goldberg. If she could find documentation proving these events actually happened, perhaps she could find existing photos as well. She might put a face to the name she'd been singing with all these months.

But would calling him by name make him anything other than a singing phantom? Could she help him move on?

And was she prepared to let him go?

"DID YOU TALK TO YOUR ACTRESS?" Yoshi asked as he stood before a grill and turned hot dogs.

Lance nursed a beer as he watched the waves of heat ripple off the coals. "My actress?"

"Last time we talked, you said you were going to see how Phoenix feels about you."

In the yard, Yoshi's girls took turns jumping on a trampoline while his wife set the outside table. Lance had already offered to help, but she'd waved him off and told him to make sure Yoshi didn't over-char the burgers.

"We still need to have that chat," Lance said. "We danced, though." A strange and magical moment that had made his heart beat out of his chest one moment and his temper flare the next.

"Danced? As in on stage or on a date?"

"On stage but after hours. She was dancing alone—just dancing, not even a rehearsal to the upcoming performance —and I joined her."

Yoshi flipped a burger. "So, did you rekindle the old flame?"

Lance pursed his lips. "Here's the thing. Initially, I thought so. We were completely under a spell, dancing as one. For a moment, I thought perhaps we could pick up where we'd left off. We could take the date we never had." He picked at the label on his glass bottle as he watched the flames lick hungrily toward the grease dripping from the meat.

"And?" Yoshi prompted.

Lance sighed. "I joined her on stage in costume, mask and cape. I rather assumed she knew it was me. We've danced before, albeit years ago. And none of the performers have my build or my voice. But at the end of the song when I took off the mask, she was genuinely surprised she'd been dancing with me."

"Who'd she think you were?" Yoshi waved his spatula in Lance's direction.

"I don't know. She ran off, and I was too miffed—at her and myself--to chase after her. I should have taken the mask off sooner, or not worn it at all. I should have talk to her before I jumped straight to kissing."

"She have a boyfriend?"

"Don't know, but the theater was closed after hours."

"Could she be dating someone else who works there? Another performer, a designer, maybe one of the office staff?" Yoshi asked.

"But who would she be confusing for me?" Lance gestured at the burgers. "You need to take those three off. They're done."

"Oh." Yoshi snatched a plate off of the small table

beside the grill and slid the patties off of the heat and onto the plate. "You haven't asked her?"

"I should," he said simply.

But the task wasn't so simple. The theater was usually bustling during the day, and he closed himself in the office at night. "I've not made the time to see her because I don't want to experience another brutal rejection," he confessed.

Yoshi dropped buns onto the grill to toast them. "Well, we're rooting for you, man. Just don't wait another eight years."

Five

P hoenix moved through the song and dance with perfectly rehearsed motions. The performers were rehearsing the *West Side Story* scene where Tony comes to Maria's balcony and they reinforce the romantic connection they made at the dance. In this run-through, the sound technician played the music through speakers without the live orchestra which they would rehearse with later.

Lance was leaning back in one of the theater chairs with his suit jacket off and his right leg propped up. He pressed a finger to his lips as he scrutinized the singing duet. Not enough chemistry.

Phoenix had done well in the run through of *I Feel Pretty*, but neither she nor her costar were projecting the passion this particular scene needed. They had to sell the fervor on stage. They needed to convince the audience that their love was bigger than life. That they were willing to risk everything to be together—familial disapproval, isolation, and disgrace.

Snapping to his feet, Lance waved his hands. "You're not showing me enough chemistry." The music stopped as he continued, "You have a love that should light up the stage. I don't want heat—I want flames. Proper fireworks, not sparklers."

In one quick motion he leaped onto the platform. "Ray, step aside."

Ray did so, giving a good-natured laugh.

"Phoenix, move to your position at the start of the song after you come down from the balcony. Cue music in three, two, one."

They launched into the song with Lance singing the part of love-struck Tony. This scene had no dancing, but it was rich with emotion. As he and Phoenix moved through their respective lyrics, he held unwavering eye contact.

The rehearsal stage faded away, as did all of the other actors and actresses. He pinned Phoenix in the moment with only his gaze, the words of the song, the melody, and the rumbling of his baritone.

They continued the scene where, unable to easily part ways, their goodbye took several minutes. They asked each other to dream of the other. Her dark amber eyes were fixed on him, and rosy cheeks accentuated her face. Lance could almost make himself believe she was a woman in love.

He felt the magic of the melody and the chemistry between them, just as he had eight years ago. The sight of her stunning wide eyes sent heat boring through his chest into his heart, and the slight parting of her lips seemed to beg for a taste of him. He held onto that moment for several long beats, burning the look of her expression into his memory.

If they hadn't been surrounded by a dozen of his subordinates, he might have taken a chance at that kiss again. But kissing wasn't part of this scene in the play. And he didn't want to push his way in as he had last time.

When they finally broke away, their captive audience clapped, and Lance had the satisfaction of knowing the fireworks between Phoenix and him were as palpable to the audience as to himself. Little did they know he wasn't acting.

He straightened his vest and regained his composure. "As you were. We'll come back to that scene. Let's take a run through America."

LANCE CLIMBED the spiral staircase up to the cupola, carrying a small electronic device. He hadn't been to the top dome of The Magnolia yet but the theater staff told him pigeons were roosting there.

When he reached the top of the stairs, he nudged the trap door open and climbed onto the platform of the intrados with a view of the city lights. He found Phoenix seated between the columns with her feet dangling over the edge. She wore the same yoga pants and shirt from rehearsal that day, and her dark hair was down.

She was looking at him over her shoulder, "Hello, Lance. You found one of my hideouts."

One?

He noted the pigeons strolling around her and a small bag of crumbs in her lap.

"Ah, so you're the culprit. Luring the rodents here."

She grinned. "There is something very cathartic about watching pigeons scurry about. What have you got there?" She jutted her chin toward the device in his hand.

He chuckled and ran a hand through his hair. "It emits a high frequency to fend off birds."

She laughed, warm and silky, startling the birds nearest her. Patting the stone ledge next to her, she offered him an invitation to sit.

He slung one leg over, then another, and took in the September night sky. The view wasn't high compared to many of New York's buildings, but it was still awe-inspiring to see the city lights from this vantage point. Then again, sitting beside Phoenix with shoulders nearly touching could have been what was stealing his breath away.

"Tell me what you have against these little creatures." She intentionally bumped shoulders with him as she tossed out the rest of her crumps onto the slanted roof.

Pigeons eagerly gobbled the food, talons clawing for purchase on the rooftop.

"Uh. They're dirty, aren't they? They poop everywhere, and they carry disease."

"I read that they don't carry any more disease than domesticated animals. They do poop everywhere, but it's probably less environmentally toxic than all the city dogs pooping and plastic bags used to pick up the mess."

"All fair points. So, are you volunteering to clean the mess up here?" He teased.

She wrinkled her nose adorably.

"Tell you what. I'll leave this little device on up here when you're not here. When you come visit your feathered friends for some avian therapy, you can just flip the switch off."

"Deal." She extended her hand.

He shook it but then didn't let it go. Keeping it in his, he settled it into his lap.

She gave a sheepish smile with flushed cheeks that had his heart racing.

"I'm glad you took the director position," she said. "We're really lucky to have you. Do you ever miss performing?"

"Sometimes. It's rewarding to see people I instruct perform well. But I do miss it sometimes. Especially when I think of how much I enjoyed performing with you. The stage always seemed more magical by your side."

Her blush turned crimson as a breeze swept hair off her shoulders. He felt the pulse on her wrist quicken. Excitement soared through him that his open feelings for her could incite a bit of anxiety in an actress who never flinched on stage.

"I missed you." She swallowed. "I like seeing you every day."

He rubbed his thumb along the hand he held. "Are you seeing anyone?" The question ended in a breath hold as his chest tightened in fear and anticipation.

"No."

He exhaled, leaning closer. How he longed to taste those ruby lips. She turned more toward him and started to close the gap.

Their lips were mere inches away when a pigeon darted between them and flew up to roost in the dome. Phoenix leaned back as the spell between them fizzled.

Lance shook his head. "See? Pests."

Phoenix laughed as she squeezed their still entwined hands. "Tell me what you've been up to all these years."

He settled in beside her, content to talk. They could take their time, he reasoned. They'd established an interest in each other, and the sparks weren't all in his head. Everything else would fall into place. It had to.

BOWMAN MET Harry at the same bench in Central Park. Autumn colors now lit the surrounding trees like wildfire—deep golden yellows, bright oranges, and vibrant reds.

Bowman leaned against the back with his legs crossed, watching Harry who sat contorted with a permanent kyphosis as he stared at birds foraging in fallen leaves.

"How is your brother?" Bowman asked.

"Not dead if that's what you're asking. I already told you I wouldn't do anything so reckless again."

No, he wouldn't, Bowman lamented, though he was shocked he'd tried to do so the first time. Harry looked like a man consumed by guilt. Bowman considered trying to console Harry, perhaps by reminding him that the former stage director hadn't been in good health to begin with. He probably shaved off less than ten years of the director's life. Besides, of all the terrible ways to die, a vasoconstrictive heart attack from a phenylephrine overdose wasn't so bad. Somehow Bowman didn't think explaining all of this to Harry would assuage his guilt. Perhaps Harry should wrestle with his conscience for a while, considering the gravity of what he'd done.

They sat in silence for several long moments. What was Harry expecting? For Bowman to offer to take out his brother? Bowman didn't kill people, not for any sum of money. His talents lay in the art of persuasion. He prided himself on being the devil on the shoulder of weaker, susceptible fools. True art resided in convincing others to bend the rules in Bowman's favor, all the while thinking the idea was their own. Harry was the first person to take Bowman's suggestions to the extreme of murder... and then botched it anyway, to no one's benefit.

"It doesn't matter anymore anyway," Harry said.

Bowman's gaze sharpened on him. "Why is that?"

"My brother and one of his actresses is applying to make the theater a historical landmark."

Red flames blurred Bowman's vision. He saw his multi-million-dollar high rise going up in smoke. There would be no tearing it down if it fell under the protective shield of New York's Landmark Preservation Commission.

"What? When?" The tedious process involved many steps. Perhaps Bowman could intervene at the public hearing or bribe someone on the LPC.

When Harry told him the voting date, his words felt like a punch to the gut. The LPC had a voting date? That meant that all of the paperwork had been filed, and the initial calendaring and public hearing had already happened.

Bowman's mind churned. Even if the LPC voted in favor, declaring the building a historical landmark had to pass the City Planning Commission or City Council. He had time to thwart the motion. But could he succeed? If he scrutinized the application form and supporting documents, he could gain a sense of how likely he would be to stop the decision to make the theater a historical building once the LPC voted.

He shook his head, frustration and anger billowed through him as his dream of owning the valuable land threatened to go up in flames. He'd invested a lot of time and energy into trying to get his hands on The Magnolia.

He stood and stormed away, needing to rid himself of his foul mood by walking through the park. "Someone should just burn the infernal thing down." The ugly thought slipped out before he could tame it. "The old theater can't be declared a historical landmark if the building no longer exists."

Six

Phoenix knocked on Lance's office door and entered the compact tidy space. A rectangular oak desk held a laptop and a few piles of papers. The shelves on either side wall had a smattering of books and a few photographs of what she assumed were family. His degree in theater hung on the wall behind the desk, but Lance wasn't here.

She heard music coming from the stage and wound her way back around to it. There, Lance danced alone to *Jet Song*. Watching his grace and fluid moves, she recalled how he'd mentioned missing performing on stage. He still possessed all that talent.

She stepped to the edge of the stage, suddenly unsure if she was taking the right course of action. With her mouth dry and heart pounding, she was shocked to realize she felt more nervous facing him than she ever did on opening night. On an exhale, she strengthened her resolve. If she could perform in front of thousands of people, she could confront one man about her feelings.

They had nearly kissed on the cupola the other night, but she hadn't yet talked to him about her strange behavior when she'd mistaken him for Gaston. She owed him an apology, which she hoped would then lead to them dating.

Taking long strides in beat to the music, she joined him.

When he saw her, he smiled and didn't miss a step. They danced toward each other, and when he offered his hands, she accepted. He spun her into a sassy, hip-swinging number before dancing around her with smooth class, like Fred Astaire.

When the song ended, she was back in his arms, heat rising from her neck into her cheeks, but he didn't move to kiss her this time.

"Thanks for joining me," he panted out the words before taking a step back and releasing her.

"The other day when we danced alone ..." she began hesitantly.

"I'm sorry if I made you uncomfortable. That wasn't my intention."

"No," she rushed to say. "I'm sorry. I was surprised and didn't handle it well. I enjoy singing and dancing with you. You may not perform anymore, but you haven't lost your touch."

His expression softened. "It's easy to perform with you. Always has been."

At his sweet words and intense gaze, her knees went rubbery. She could melt onto the floor in a puddle, but that would be counterproductive to her reason for coming to see him.

"I feel the same way about you," she said.

His smile widened as he took a step closer to her. "I like

the sound of that. I'm attracted to you, Phoenix. When you pushed me away after our last dance, I thought perhaps you were dating someone. Then on the dome you said you weren't, and the night felt perfect by your side."

"Perfect," she agreed.

He reached down and took her hand in his. A burst of possibilities raced through her mind. Fate had distanced them but now drew them back together. During the years separating them, she thought she'd been clinging to a fairy tale. Maybe she had romanticized the chemistry between them in her mind, and all of the passion of the musicals she performed had disconnected her from reality.

Yet, here they were. Holding hands and feeling the electric attraction dance between them. She felt the same buildup to the kiss that she had the other night, except now there were no pigeons to intervene.

She arched up toward him.

A rapping on the audience floor startled both of them.

She turned to see who had intruded on her moment. "Cillian."

"Mr. Byrne." Lance squeezed her hand before releasing it and stepping back.

She suspected he wouldn't want his affections to be mistaken for attempting to seduce one of the actresses, since he held a position of relative power.

"Lovely dance. Too bad it isn't part of the show." With his portable oxygen concentrator slung over one shoulder, he ambled with a cane.

Lance nimbly hopped off the stage and Phoenix followed.

"I'm here for an update and forecast." Cillian took a

seat in the first row of audience chairs. If he'd noticed them fraternizing, he didn't let on.

Phoenix knew Cillian was asking about the financial outlook of the theater and not the weather. Since she had a vested interest both emotionally, in the time she'd spent working to try to make it a historical site, and financially, since this was her livelihood, she took a seat beside Cillian. If he had something to discuss he didn't want her to hear, he would have to ask her to leave.

He didn't.

Lance adjusted his vest as he leaned against the railings. "Projections are good. We need three-quarters capacity every night to cover expenses—salaries, props, utilities, repairs. We have that opening night. After that, we're at fifty percent, but with last minute bookings and walk-ins, I'm quite confident we'll reach our target."

Cillian rested his hand on the armrest. "Good. Good. You should also be aware that Phoenix has been working to make the building a designated historical site."

"Oh. Will that affect the performances?" Lance asked.

"No," Phoenix assured him. "It will just add prestige. After the theater district declined in the 1970s, there a big push to preserve Broadway theaters in the eighties. Twenty-five were declared landmarks following the initial petition for forty-four of them, and The Magnolia wasn't one of them."

After that, Disney themed musicals like *The Lion King* and *Beauty and the Beast* infused more audiences into theaters for the next five decades. But The Magnolia was a smaller scale building and couldn't draw revenue like the larger theaters. She didn't mind working for a smaller production, even if it meant pulling a smaller salary.

"Why not all forty-four?" Lance asked.

"Some owners fought making them landmarks, because that designation meant they couldn't demolish the theater and sell the plot or vice versa."

"Making The Magnolia a landmark also means that after I die, it can't be torn down," Cillian added. "Ownership rights can be transferred, but no demolition can take place."

Phoenix winced. She didn't like the way he spoke so casually about death, although he'd told her once he'd made his peace with it.

Lance's brow furrowed. "Someone wants to tear down The Magnolia?"

Cillian explained. "Developers are after the plot for new construction—have been for years. When their attempt to throw money at me failed, they coerced my brother, Harry. He's tried begging, pleading, and threatening me, but his antics have fallen on deaf ears. Perhaps quite literally, since I'm losing my hearing thanks to these cursed water pills I'm taking."

"So, if you make it a historical building, your brother can't sell it to developers. Or he can," Lance amended, "but they can't tear down the theater."

"Exactly. In the meantime, I'm counting on you to keep her financially afloat."

Lance took two steps to stand beside Phoenix. He smiled down at her as he took her hand. "We can do that."

She wondered if he understood how much The

Magnolia meant to her. He seemed to be promising her he would do his best as much as he was promising Cillian.

THE CROWDS CAME, and the seats filled.

Phoenix spent her days hydrating and her evenings performing. This was a busy time for Lance, who fulfilled many roles for Cillian, so Phoenix gave him the space to work. Backstage, he would wink at her with heat in his eyes, conveying his ongoing interest despite the hectic schedule. They had set a day and time for that elusive date, so she resolved to patiently wait.

Amidst her cycle of performances, she hadn't spent any time with Gaston. Surely, the ghost would understand; he had, after all, been in show business himself. She'd researched his demise after hearing the story of Charles Goldberg and could finally put a face to the voice. The black and white newspaper photo at the New York Public Library for Performing Arts showed a broad-shouldered man with light hair and a square jaw. The gleaming smile contrasted with the tragedy that befell him.

Backstage, she slipped into her dress for the scene where Marie sings, "I Feel Pretty."

Carrie straightened her hem. "When are you and Lance going to consummate this thing you've got going on?"

"Is it that obvious?"

Carrie rolled her eyes as she turned away to preen her hair in a nearby mirror. "The crowd can probably sense it."

"We have a date tomorrow night."

"The two of you have an undeniable sizzle. And you

share a passion for theater. I hope it works out." Her blue-eyed gaze darted to Phoenix then back to the mirror.

"Why do you say it like that?" Phoenix checked her own hair in the mirror.

"I don't want to give up either of you if it doesn't. He's the best stage director I've ever worked with, and you're my best friend."

Phoenix tilted her head with a smile. "Don't worry. I've been waiting a long time for Lance Hamilton. We both want a relationship."

Phoenix swayed slightly, and Carrie stood with alarm on her face. "Are you okay?"

"Yeah, good." The room, which had seemed to tilt, straightened. Maybe she hadn't hydrated enough earlier that day. She could remedy that between scenes. A small voice in her mind reminded her that she'd had a few such spells over the last few days.

"Swooning at the thought of sir Lancelot?"

Phoenix managed a smile. "Something like that."

PHOENIX PUT a hand to her forehead. Was it suddenly warm? She didn't feel well. Her unsettled stomach churned, and fatigue had her wanting to crawl into bed and take a nap, perhaps for the next several days. Was it something she'd eaten? Except, she'd been gradually feeling more run down over the last week, suggesting that whatever this was, it was more insidious than food poisoning. Some type of viral infection perhaps?

She'd probably run her immune system into the ground

with long nights of performance. Tonight's show had gone spectacularly. Now that she had time to rest, her body wanted to simply collapse. She told herself she just needed more water. The idea of missing a performance—of missing that date—knotted her stomach more than the dizziness did.

She was supposed to have a date with Lance tomorrow night and wondered if she'd feel well enough to see him. Rest tonight, date tomorrow.

But first, she wanted to visit Gaston before she went home. After changing out of her costume into jeans and a T-shirt, she walked barefoot down the stone steps into the chamber room. The surface felt smooth and cool against her burning skin.

Why was she so feverish? Maybe if she just spent a few hours down here in the cool, moist air cool, she would feel better.

She lit a multitude of candles encircling the room before walking to the center. Then the voice began. Gaston sang *Music of the Night*—a perfect selection from *The Phantom of the Opera*.

Too weak to join him in singing, she sat on the cold mosaic tiled floor and let the melody sweep her into a trance. His voice flowed like satin over her skin, calming and soothing. Her body reacted with a shiver, and she marveled at how she simultaneously felt feverish and chilled.

The candle flames danced around her, as if they were controlled by Gaston's singing. They grew taller and shorter, mimicking the notes of the song. The stones seemed to close around her, a cool cage of echoing sound.

She closed her eyes and imagined she heard the sound of the violin accompanying the lyrics.

Everything about her interaction with the ghost was positively magical. She pushed away the small voice in her head suggesting her infatuation wasn't healthy. How could the magic of the music she shared with Gaston bring her such pleasure, ease all of her troubles, and be bad for her?

No. Listening to him and embracing his voice would heal her soul. She joined him in singing.

LANCE FINISHED LOOKING over the finances of the weeks' earnings on his laptop and closed down the electronic device.

His phone rang.

"Nana, what a pleasant surprise!"

"No, Lance. Something is wrong. I told you she would need you. And now she does."

His stomach knotted at the intensity of his grandmother's voice. He knew that tone from previous premonitions she'd had. He gripped the phone tighter. "What are you talking about?"

"Where is she? Where is the bird? She's in her cage."

Had she just answered her own question?

Bird? "What bird?"

"She stays in her cage, but not for long. You can find her."

"Nana—"

She cut him off. "Stop talking to me and find her." She disconnected the call.

Lance stared at his phone. If he didn't know his grandmother better, he'd have thought some type of age-related delirium had set in. But he couldn't dismiss her worry.

Bird?

Phoenix.

After jumping to his feet, his hands shook as he scrolled for her phone. He dialed her phone. No answer.

She's in her cage.

What cage?

Not her apartment. That wouldn't make any sense. He walked the hallway from one end to the other, mind racing. The theater was empty this late after the show.

Bird in a cage.

Surely the stage wasn't her cage. The stage was her freedom. Her open air.

Not the cupola, since that was a rooftop view and not a cage.

Lance stilled, feeling a cold breeze from down the hallway. He followed it as the hair on his neck stood on end. The peculiar coolness emanated from the storage closet. He opened the door only to find another open door—a secret door the same texture as the wall, and he wouldn't have known it was there if not for being carelessly left open.

"Phoenix? Are you down here, love?"

He heard no answer.

He stepped through the doorway and into the darkness beyond. Crisp air enveloped him. When his eyes adjusted to the dimness, he noted stairs that descended to a flickering light in the distance. Was he on a wild goose chase, or could this place be called a cage?

Perhaps it was one of her hiding spots.

Following his instincts, he descended the stairs.

The scene he came upon mystified him and rendered him utterly speechless. A barefooted Phoenix sat in the center of a room wearing a pair of blue jeans and a T-shirt. On a ledge surrounding her in a complete circle burned several dozen fierce candles. They weren't the steady, lazy burn of normal candles. These flames danced as if to music.

With Phoenix in the center, eyes closed, she looked like she might be captivated in a séance.

When she stood, Lance drew in a sharp breath thinking she'd spotted him. He didn't want her to accuse him of intruding on her personal time. But her eyes remained closed.

He moved into the shadow against the wall to continue to watch her. She looked pale and frail, but began to sing *The Phantom of the Opera's*, "All I Ask of You." He didn't want to barge in, lest he be met with the same incredulity as when he'd danced with her in the mask. Yet, they'd moved passed that, hadn't they?

Lance stood, mesmerized by the dancing flames around Phoenix. The candlelight moved as though it was some type of sound spectrogram, growing longer and shorter in rhythmic synchrony.

Her voice sounded so beautiful, like an angel. But she wasn't well. She sang with a slight raspy infiltration to her singing—a breathlessness more like a broken angel. He thought she'd looked ill on stage today, but now he could see she was undeniably sick. In fact, wasting away. As she swayed, her voice and her body appeared more petite.

Too worried about her to watch in the shadows any longer, he stepped into the circle of light. "Phoenix."

She turned toward him, eyes glazed and half-moon dark circles beneath them. Her skin had a thin sheen of sweat.

She gave him a soft smile before collapsing into his arms. As she did so, the surrounding candles shrunk to small flames, seemingly representative of the small, feverish body he held his arms.

Seven

Lance sat in the chair beside the hospital bed where Phoenix slept. A clear bag hung from a pole dripping hydrating fluid into her. She had already gotten intravenous antibiotics, and the admitting physician had explained that Phoenix suffered from walking pneumonia.

In the twelve hours that had passed since she'd collapsed in his arms, he'd brought her to the emergency room, she was evaluated and admitted, and he'd notified both his grandmother and Phoenix's sister, Jenny, of her condition.

Jenny had vowed to take the next direct flight from Charlotte to LaGuardia, and Lance suspected she would be at the hospital soon.

When Phoenix's eyes fluttered open, Lance's heart skipped a beat. The fatigue that had been tugging at his eyelids instantly vanished. He moved to the side of the bed and took her hand, expecting he would need to re-orient her since she'd spent most of the last twelve hours sleeping.

They were in a small room with a dingy window letting

in light and giving a view of nothing but a brick wall where the building made an L shape.

"Phoenix, you're in the hospital."

She looked up at him, blinking in confusion.

He touched a hand to her forehead, relieved to find her fever had broken. She'd drenched her sheets in sweat, and her dark hair was moist and stringy. Her eyes had lost their haunted look from the chamber and now conveyed to him that she was going to pull through.

When he'd described the situation he'd found her in—alone in the cold chamber—the doctor had suggested Lance had saved her life. The physician added that cool room probably kept Phoenix's fever from spiking too high, and if she'd simply gone home alone and went to bed, the infection might have overwhelmed her body.

Lance didn't understand what happened down in that chamber—Phoenix's eerie singing and the way the candles had acted of their own accord. But questions about those circumstances could wait until Phoenix was better.

"Lance, what are you doing here?"

"I had to bring you to a hospital. You're properly unwell—pneumonia." He didn't add that when she'd passed out in the chamber, she'd drained about five years off his life.

"Pneumonia?" She struggled to sit up, looking down at the IV in her arm and touching a hand to the nasal cannula on her face delivering oxygen.

He reached for the bed controls and elevated the head of the bed. "Let me help you."

"I remember singing. And then you were there." She

reached up and touched a hand to his face. "You were glowing from the candlelight."

He might've melted under her touch if he hadn't been so infuriated with her for taxing her body ruthlessly to the point of collapse. "The doctor said you wore yourself down through overworking and under eating. Now it's forcing you to take it easy."

Lance would make sure Phoenix listened to her body. He'd never known the agony of watching someone he cared about fall ill followed by enduring horrible hours of not knowing what sort of recovery was expected.

"Pneumonia," she repeated. "Seems like such a medieval thing to have."

His mouth quirked. "I didn't say the plague, love."

"I'm sorry about all of this, especially at the start of show season."

"Don't worry about that now. You need to rest," he told her.

She withdrew her hand, leaned back on the pillow, and stared up at the ceiling.

He took her hand back and held it with both of his. "You scared me. So did the internet when I looked it up—apparently fifty thousand people die in the States every year from pneumonia." He kissed the back of her hand. "I'm glad that's not you."

When she smiled, her face looked a little less drained. "We have something special, you and I. Now that we've finally acknowledged that and stopped tap dancing around each other, I'm not going anywhere."

He kissed the back of her hand by way of agreeing with her.

. . .

A KNOCK SOUNDED on the hospital room door, and Phoenix looked up to see her sister enter the room.

"Jenny!"

Jenny brushed by Lance with a brief but heartfelt, "Thank you for calling me," before embracing Phoenix in a hug.

Joy spread through Phoenix at the sight and comfort filled her. The sensation was immediately followed by guilt that her illness had drawn Jenny from a busy attorney practice.

As Jenny pulled away, Phoenix wondered how atrocious she must look compared to Jenny's tidiness. Her sister wore a fitted brown suit with pumps as if she were going to court. They looked vastly different—Jenny with long blonde hair and tan skin from weekends on the golf course and Phoenix with pale skin like their father and wavy, dark hair.

Lance left the room murmuring something about fetching tea.

Jenny looked over her shoulder, watching him go. "Tea?" She turned back to Phoenix. "How very British of him," she said lightly.

"I think he saved my life," Phoenix said.

"Tell me what happened," Jenny said.

Phoenix fidgeted with the white hospital blanket, feeling very much like the younger sister under scrutiny. "The show has been a lot of work and stress. Seems I haven't been eating and sleeping well. My defenses were weakened, and I got pneumonia."

"You didn't tell me you were sick."

"I didn't know. Not really." Phoenix said. "I've mostly been fatigued for a few days and a little lightheaded from time to time. I guess that's why they call it walking pneumonia."

Jenny pursed her lips. "I'm glad you're on the road to recovery. Lance scared me when he called and described your condition." She pulled the hospital chair closer to the bed and sat down.

"So," Phoenix changed the subject, "show me the ring."

Her sister had gotten engaged a few weeks ago and had told Phoenix over the phone, but she'd yet to see the ring in person.

With a twinge of self-consciousness, Jenny extended her hand.

"Opulent!" Phoenix appraised the princess cut set in white gold.

"Beau defended the jeweler's niece on a tax fraud case, so he got a good deal."

"It's gorgeous. I'm so happy for you."

"He's fantastic. We play golf on the weekends, and Friday night is game night with his son Travis. During the week, we catch lunch together when we can at this little restaurant near the courthouse." Jenny's expression glowed as she talked about the man she would spend the rest of her life with.

Lance returned. "Thought we could all do with a cuppa," he said, handing over the paper cups.

After thanking him, Jenny turned back to Phoenix. "Are you feeling better?"

"Tired, but that was mostly how I felt leading up to this point."

"Lance said he found you in the tunnels beneath the theater."

Phoenix's gaze slid to him and back to Jenny. She'd probably looked like she was doing some type of ritual, standing in the middle of a chamber adorned with candles. Unless he was a medium too, he wouldn't have heard the beautiful music from Gaston that she'd heard.

Jenny narrowed her eyes at Phoenix. "I don't think your relationship with that ghost is healthy."

"Gaston didn't give me pneumonia," Phoenix shot back. "He was trying to warn me though." She wrapped her hands around her tea, hugging the warm cup as she avoided making eye contact with Lance.

"Who is Gaston?" he asked.

Phoenix didn't answer as her cheeks burned. She would be forced to tell Lance about her serenading phantom, and then their fragile relationship would shatter like a champagne flute on stone.

Was it so tenuous? They both seemed driven to build a relationship despite the obstacles they continued to encounter. But could they share one capable of withstanding the paranormal?

"A ghost, I'm guessing."

All eyes turned to a round woman in the doorway with silver hair. She wore a purple floral dress and a beige cardigan.

"Nana," Lance stammered out the word in surprise as he stepped over to give her a peck on the cheek. "What are you doing here?" he asked, voice baffled but kind.

"Well, you're absolute amateurs, aren't you?" She spoke to Phoenix and Jenny with an amused British accent. "When you remember your manners, Lance dear, please introduce me."

Phoenix cracked a smile at Lance's reddening cheeks.

"Nana, this is Phoenix Wiley and her sister Jenny. This is my grandmother, Pauline."

"Charming. Always a delight to meet other mediums. Are you the first in the family, or did one of your parents have the ability?"

Phoenix swallowed against a dry throat. She glanced at Lance who looked dumbstruck but not as though he struggled to keep pace with the topic of conversation. "Our father."

"Oh, very good. It's more of a shock to those with no prior knowledge of the paranormal," Pauline said.

Jenny scrutinized Lance. "Can you interact with ghosts?"

"No, I haven't that ability. We've always known Nana had ... unusual skills. Are you saying you can see ghosts?"

"We're not admitting to anything," Jenny said.

Phoenix supposed that was a rather lawyerly response.

Pauline frowned. "Whether you care to admit to any dealings with the paranormal or not, you're in danger, Phoenix Wiley. Best we put aside the fact we're strangers and start working together to learn why ghosts are warning both of us that you're in danger—and, I suspect, not just from pneumonia."

A long stretch of silence hung in the room. Phoenix couldn't bring herself to look at Lance.

He shifted his weight. "Listen, I don't know anything

about ghosts." He stepped forward and took Phoenix's hand. "But if Nana believes there's danger, then it exists. I'd never forgive myself if something happened to you because we didn't take steps to prevent it. I want to be part of the solution. I want to help. I won't shy away from the bizarre if it means abandoning you. Please let Nana help if she thinks she can."

The warmth from his hand flowed through Phoenix. Her gaze trailed from their joined hands, up his strong arms, to the overgrowth on his jaw, and settled on his dark eyes. She could lose herself in those compassionate eyes. She wanted to be back on stage, dancing in his arms with their hearts beating as one.

"Okay." She gave a soft smile as she squeezed his hand in return. "I've been hearing a ghost in the cavern beneath the theater. Only hearing, never seeing. And he sings—beautifully, magnificently, longingly. For months, I've gone down those stairs to listen to him sing. Sometimes, we sing together. I called him Gaston because he would never tell me his name."

"Gaston Leroux?" Lance asked.

Phoenix smiled at him. "Yes, exactly."

Lance explained to his grandmother, "He wrote *The Phantom of the Opera* in 1910." Turning back to Phoenix, he quoted Leroux, "'*Our lives are one masked ball.*'"

Phoenix kissed the back of his hand and turned to look at Pauline. "In my research to save The Magnolia and make it a historical landmark, I learned about the history of the theater. During prohibition it served as both a theater and distillery with distribution tunnels. The leading lady was caught in a love triangle with the obsessive mafia's henchman who owned the distillery and the leading actor whom she loved. She stepped in front of the bullet meant for her lover. Not long after, he died on stage of a broken heart. His name was Charles Goldberg."

Words from Leroux's novel surfaced in her mind. '*I am dying of love,*' the Phantom of the Opera had cried. '*I am dying of love for her, I tell you.*'

Phoenix shuddered. "If I'm right, then Charles Goldberg is our phantom—a real phantom."

"And the dangerous part?" Jenny asked.

Phoenix shook her head. "I'm not sure. His voice has gained an urgency and an edge. I don't know why."

"Why couldn't it be the pneumonia?" Lance asked, glancing at his grandmother as he continued to hold Phoenix's hand.

"No," Pauline said. "You've saved her from that, Lance, but there's something else or the spirits wouldn't have told me to come here. We need to ask Phoenix's phantom."

"He doesn't speak, only sings," Phoenix said.

"Then we must listen to him sing."

Eight

Lance and his grandmother left Phoenix to rest under Jenny's care at the hospital. He and Nana took a cab back to his apartment.

On the way, he called Carrie and checked on the theater.

"Mary will do a great job," she reassured him.

Lance had no doubt that Phoenix's understudy knew the role well. Still, nerves in performing for a large audience could discombobulate even the most accomplished actors.

"How is Phoenix?" Carrie asked.

"Better compared to when I brought her to the hospital. I don't have a timeframe for when she'll be ready to perform again."

"No rush. I mean, we all miss her, but she needs to get well first."

"I'll keep you posted, and I'll be at tonight's performance."

When he hung up the phone, he turned toward his grandmother. "I can't believe you traveled all the way from

71

England to New York. And without calling me. Was your flight okay?"

The cab pulled to the curb where they exited and Lance hauled her suitcase toward his apartment.

"The trip went well."

He held the door open. "I'm glad you came. I'm way out of my depth here." He tried to wrap his head around the concept of the woman he adored being able to hear ghosts. He'd certainly felt an eerie, other-worldly presence in the underground room.

They walked to the elevator, where he pushed the button.

Lance continued. "Something paranormal lurks down in that chamber. When I found Phoenix, the candle flames were... dancing. She looked like a ghost herself—so pale."

They stepped into the elevator, riding it up to the eighth floor.

"When she collapsed in my arms, the flames practically extinguished, as if a reflection of her health. Even talking about it gives me chills."

"She's alive because of you," Nana said.

Without Nana's warning, Lance wouldn't have known to go looking for Phoenix. She was the real hero here.

"Yet still in danger according to you," he complained as he unlocked his door and let them inside his apartment. "I'll make up the spare bed for you."

"Tomorrow, Phoenix will be discharged. After that, we'll go to the theater and meet this singing shade."

Lance pulled a bottle of sparkling water from his fridge, twisted off the cap, and handed it to Nana. "So soon? Will she be well enough for that?"

"Your little bird won't be taking flight until she's mended, but a little excursion won't set her back. Besides, you'll be there to look after her." She accepted the bottle and took a long drink. "Right, then. Let's have a cuppa. Settle our nerves."

He filled a kettle with water and set it on the stove.

"Do you like her?" he asked, trying to sound casual, but they both knew how much he valued Nana's opinion.

"What's not to like? She's a good heart, that one. Trying to save the theater. She's quite lovely, and she's obviously enamored with you."

He fumbled with the teacups as he took them out of the cupboard. They clattered on the counter before he steadied them. "She is?"

"Don't be daft," she teased. "And I don't need a spirit to tell me what's plain as day in her eyes."

He glanced at Nana, wondering how she could see Phoenix's feelings without ever having met her before. "The feeling's mutual. I think we have a real chance at a relationship this time around."

But doubt crept into his mind. They had a real chance, unless fate drew them apart again. He wouldn't let that happen, but if something tragic and permanent struck, as it almost had in the cavern, what could he do?

"What do you suppose the danger is?" he asked.

"I haven't the faintest idea. We must remain alert for anything."

He'd nearly lost her once. The idea of facing that fear again made his pulse trip.

∽

BOWMAN TUCKED his napkin in his lap even though he knew he wouldn't eat—couldn't eat—as Silas gorged on two overstuffed beef burritos. He'd already eaten half the chips and salsa along with a jumbo margarita. Where did it all go?

Silas was beginning to feel like a charity case since Bowman paid and fed him once a week. The boy wasn't rail thin anymore, still had that baby face though. Bowman's scheming to seize the theater would end one day, and he wondered if he'd miss their meals together, listening to Silas's innocent rambling.

"So then Carrie was taking a shower and the pipe burst," Silas said around a mouthful of rice and beans. "Lance fixed it—I mentioned he's the new director. I think he's been doing little side jobs to keep the theater patched up. The building's so old. Some of the performers even think it's haunted with its flickering lights and weird drafts." He gulped his margarita to wash down another shovel-full of food. "I think it adds to the mysteriousness."

"Or adds to the efforts to make it a historical building," Bowman grumbled.

"Yeah, I heard people talking about that. Phoenix filed some paperwork for it."

Bowman's mind had been wandering at the rambling but snapped back to attention. "*She's* making it a historical building? That sounds industrious." He thought of the names he'd researched when looking for his target—his future spy. He remembered the name Phoenix because it had struck him as unusual. She was one of the lead actresses, and Silas continually spoke highly of her.

Silas shrugged. "It's, like, her pet project. Everybody's

got one. Lance is doing repairs. Phoenix is researching. Lee and Ray are restoring old costumes. My pet project is talking to you."

"There are a lot of steps to making a building a historical landmark. I hope she has help," Bowman lied.

"Her sister's a lawyer. She's helping, I think. And Carrie has as aunt on the preservation committee, so maybe she'll succeed."

"But Phoenix is leading the efforts to make The Magnolia a historical landmark?"

"Yeah. She's doing all the heavy lifting." Silas chomped on a chip dripping with salsa.

Phoenix, Bowman mulled over the name. He wondered if an angle to play her existed. Probably not if she was the type of person who spent her free time doing the tedious paperwork and research required to pass a building through the LPC with no direct expectation of her own financial reward. He might need someone to put her out of commission before she succeeded.

Everyone had enemies, especially leading ladies.

He wondered if the sentimental old man, Cillian, had put her up to the work of submitting to the LPC, since Harry was the one who'd first mentioned the move to declare The Magnolia a historical building.

"Phoenix is sick though," Silas added, his voice becoming doleful. "Carrie said she's in the hospital with pneumonia. We sent her a card and flowers, and Lance had the understudy taking over her role as Maria."

Pneumonia. As promising as that sounded, an acute illness wasn't going to stop a young woman for long. Could he turn this into a more permanent incapacitation for her?

He contemplated the ways as he watched Silas polish off his meal but was surprised to discover his heart felt uncommitted to ruining a young life.

And all of the possibilities led to a maze of infinite other possibilities. The tragic incapacitation of a young actress might only create a host of followers willing to finish what she'd started. Making a pseudo-martyr of her wouldn't help him get the theater.

No, Bowman would need to think of another way to get his hands on the theater. But what did that mean for Silas? Unemployment? And why did Bowman care? He shook off the sentimentality.

The kid looked up at him with a lopsided smile of crooked teeth and rosy cheeks. "Thanks for the lunch, Mr. B."

"No problem."

"Say, all we do is talk about my stuff. What about you?"

"What about me?"

"You're married." Silas gestured to the ring on Bowman's finger. "You got a family?"

He looked down at the ring and turned it slowly. "Had a family," he said. He'd drifted apart from his wife over the years, and they no longer lived together.

Silas's brow furrowed. "Sorry, man. My sister miscarried a few years back. Really devastated her."

Bowman lifted his gaze, surprised by the way Silas's sincerity touched him. "My son would have been about your age. He had cerebral palsy and developed complications. He was bed bound with contractions and suffered many infections."

"That's awful."

"We gave him what quality of life we could for as long as we could." He shocked himself by confiding these things in Silas. Normally, he never talked about his son. It just wasn't done—was too painful to do.

"Tell me more about your family." Genuinely interested, Bowman picked up his fish taco and took a bite.

～

PHOENIX HELD a pot of daisies from her coworkers as Jenny unlocked her apartment and let them inside.

"I'm glad you're going home so soon, but are you sure you're okay? You look a little pale."

"The stairs were taxing."

"You need to take your time before going back to work. And whatever other activity you have planned with Lance." Jenny closed the door behind them, giving her sister a wink.

Phoenix set the flowers on her kitchen table. "We've actually never done anything together outside of the workplace."

"That's disappointing. He obviously cares about you. And you get all doe-eyed looking at him."

Phoenix fixed herself a glass of water. "We're passionate about theater, and passionate about each other. Everything else will take time and exploration."

Jenny jiggled the prescription bottle of antibiotics they'd picked up from the pharmacy on the way home and set it down on the counter. "He's looking out for you, and that goes a long way in my book. He's not bolting at the mention of spirits, so he also scores bonus points there. After all, Beau wasn't easily convinced when I told him the ghost of the murder victim whose case we were trying to solve was in the car with us."

"Yes, one less hurdle is nice," Phoenix agreed. "Now, we have a seance to do."

"Not today," Jenny said pointedly. She'd already put her foot down when Phoenix and Pauline started the discussion that morning. "You need to recover from pneumonia first. The only reason I agreed to let you go to the theater tomorrow is because I'm leaving the day after that and I want to hear this phantom of yours. But don't push yourself too hard."

"I'll be fine." Phoenix waved a dismissive hand at her older sister as she drank her water. Truth be told, she didn't mind having Jenny here and fussing over her a little.

"And we need to get some meat on those bones."

"There's a Greek place two blocks from here," Phoenix suggested.

"Mmm. Souvlaki?"

"Yes. Yum. Their baklava is heavenly." Thinking about the thin phyllo dough layered with pistachios and honey had her mouth watering.

"Done," Jenny said. "I'll be back. Bolt the door behind me."

And there it is, Phoenix thought as Jenny left, this strange lingering threat of danger Gaston had conveyed through his singing, reinforced by Lance's grandmother traveling across the Atlantic because she sensed something sinister too. They needed to resolve this mysterious, shadowy danger so everyone could stop worrying about her.

Nine

All was quiet in the early morning hour outside the theater except the sound of his key sliding in the lock. Lance held the door as Nana, Jenny, and Phoenix walked through it. Rather than taking the back employee entrance, he escorted everyone through the front. He wanted his grandmother to see the beauty of The Magnolia.

The door closed on squeaking hinges, automatically locking again to the outside, but anyone wishing to exit need only push the center bar to release the locking mechanism.

The four of them made their way beyond the entrance, past the stairs to the balcony level, and toward the rear seating as Lance tuned on the lights. The theater wouldn't officially open for another four hours.

"Oh, Lance," Nana began, "it's so beautiful."

Audience seating comprised four sections of one hundred plush red seats each. The balcony level with prime viewing had three sections trimmed with ornately carved banisters. In front of the stage spread a partially concealed pit for the symphony. Enormous curtains framed the large platform.

He offered Nana his arm and escorted her down the aisle. They looped around backstage.

Nana wrinkled her nose. "That's a bit pungent."

"The paint smell? Yeah, we're renovating back here, and the ventilation isn't great," he explained. "We open doors and run fans to intermittently aerate the place."

They walked to the closet where Phoenix opened the secret door. Cool air and darkness greeted them.

"I'm amazed you found this place," Jenny said.

Phoenix shrugged. "I never would have without the singing. Took me all night to carve a rectangle in the wood panels to release the door behind them."

"What about you?" Jenny asked Lance.

"I followed the chilly draft and creepy, eerie sensation."

"You weren't scared?" Jenny asked.

"Of what?" He chuckled. "Monsters in the dark? The young boy in every man dreams of finding a secret room, a hidden portal, or a long-forgotten chamber."

It felt more like a portal, he thought, as they descended the stairs, holding their phone flashlights in front of them and walking over stone laid a hundred years ago. They seemed to be transported back in time, as if they might emerge on the other side to the roaring twenties with women in shag dresses and men in fedoras.

At the bottom of the stairs, they walked forward into a large chamber—the one where Phoenix had collapsed in his arms a few days ago. She picked up a match box and went around the circle of candles, lighting them.

Lance, Jenny, and Nana each grabbed a lit candle and helped set the others aflame. The act felt ritualistic to Lance, even though he was apparently the only one in the group who couldn't see or hear ghosts.

When they finished, the four of them stood in a circle of light. Beyond the glow hovered a rim of darkness. The last time he'd been here, he'd watched Phoenix sing and sway. Now, his eyes scanned the edge of darkness, and he wondered what lay beyond. How big was the chamber, and were there other access points? There must be tunnels connected to the room if a network had been used to smuggle alcohol in addition to distilling it. Perhaps he could explore more later when he wasn't with a group of ghost summoners.

Phoenix took his hand and leaned against him. "Now we see if he'll perform for a crowd."

Nana took a deep breath and lifted her arms. "Charles Goldberg, we are here to help you cross over into the light. We will help you find peace." After a moment, she said, "He's singing."

Lance felt like the odd man out. Everyone could hear the voice except him, yet the hair on the back of his neck stood on end as the candle flames swayed. Even though he didn't hear the ghost, he could feel a strange presence.

Phoenix squeezed his hand. "It's beautiful. I haven't heard this song before. It isn't from a musical. It's about fear of love and facing new beginnings. The chorus is about a phoenix rising out of the ashes."

He stood with the three women, watching the candles

dance with amazement and wondering about the purpose of all this. Would the ghost cross—move on from haunting the physical world and Phoenix? Or would he confirm that Phoenix was in some other danger?

Lance would do whatever it took to keep her safe. If a seance was required, so be it. He never again wanted to be holding her in his arms as she looked to be on death's door.

The candles dimmed.

"It's ended," Nana said. "He's not ready to move on. There's still danger."

"What danger?" Lance pulled Phoenix closer to him.

"He didn't specify," Phoenix said. "Gaston was singing about a phoenix."

Jenny raked fingers through her blonde hair. "His tone sounded edgy, but are we reading too much into it? On the other hand, I don't want to be flippant or dismissive of warnings from ghosts. They sometimes know things about the future."

"Predictions," Nana agreed.

"I'm getting better from the pneumonia," Phoenix said. "What danger could I possibly be in?"

"A jealous colleague," Jenny began, "ex-boyfriend, rogue fan."

"I don't think I have any of those."

"Safety in numbers," Nana said. "I'm inclined to think it's related to the theater because that is the ghost's domain, but we shouldn't assume that. You shouldn't be alone."

"I'll stay with Phoenix when she's at the theater," Lance said, kissing the top of her forehead.

"And I'll stay at the apartment," Jenny said.

"You have to get back to your day job," Phoenix protested. "You can't stay with me indefinitely."

"You can stay with me," Lance offered. "I have a spare bedroom."

"You have Pauline," Phoenix said, looking up at him.

"I'll sleep on the couch," he said.

"We don't know how long this will take." Frustration reared in her voice.

Clearly, she didn't want to inconvenience everyone based on the speculation of a threat, Lance thought.

He assured her, "I'm fairly sure whatever the danger is, the ghost wouldn't go through the trouble of warning you months in advance."

"I don't want to burden you."

He gave her a soft, reassuring smile. "You could never be a burden."

"He's right," Nana said. "Danger is probably eminent. You won't be displaced from your home for long."

Phoenix looked around at the faces as though realizing they weren't going to settle for less than twenty-four-hour surveillance. "Okay. I'll stay with Lance until this ends— either Gaston gives us the all clear or the danger rears its ugly head."

BOWMAN TOOK a sip of his champagne. After setting the glass down on the elevated table, he straightened the cuff of his tuxedo.

Is this what his life had become? Schmoozing with the city's wealthy to grease the wheels as a developer? Well, at least he was good at it. In addition, he built homes and businesses; his work was important for the people of the city—roofs over their heads and paychecks in their bank accounts.

Still, part of him wanted to be lounging at home, beer in hand. Or maybe having a meal with Silas while he talked about the love of his life—the theater.

"What do you want out of life, Mr. B?"

Silas's question had been simple enough. Bowman supposed he wanted what most people did—to matter. He made himself matter via the work he did. Perhaps. Or perhaps that was his ego talking.

His conversations with Silas were jumbling his thoughts. This kid with little money found happiness in the simplest things in life—coworkers, movies, and meals with a stranger. His innocence was both mind boggling and intriguing.

When Bowman's phone vibrated, he dug it out of his pocket. "Hello."

"I did it." Harry's voice sounded high-pitched, almost maniacal.

Bowman's blood ran cold as ice. "Did what?" He started to make his way toward the exit of the convention center ballroom.

"It's going to burn down. It won't become a historical landmark." Harry sounded like a greedy kid waiting for his father's approval.

Bowman's mouth tasted like sawdust. He flashed back to the last time he'd been with Harry; he'd been thinking aloud about an incident which would help him get the property. He never meant that he actually wanted Harry to burn it down.

"What did you do?" Bowman demanded, making his way outside where cars, busses, and taxis zipped by the curb.

"It's okay. I started it in the costume room near an outlet. It'll look like an electrical fire."

Bowman checked his watch. Silas had said that some people stayed late to work on the set or costumes. "Harry, you idiot!" But he didn't have time to give him a tongue-lashing.

"But—"

Bowman hung up the phone as he hailed a taxi. His mind thought of everything flammable in the theater—costumes, props, old wood. Silas said repairs were ongoing so there would be sealant and paint.

He climbed into the cab, barking out the address as he dialed Silas's number.

"Mr. B, how are you?" His voice was all youthful jubilance.

"Where are you?"

"What's wrong, Mr. B?"

"Where?"

"At the theater. Why do you sound upset?"

"Get out of there now. Get everyone out!"

"Okay. Okay."

"Is there a fire alarm?" Bowman demanded.

"Yeah. Bunch of them."

"Pull it and leave."

"Yeah, okay. Okay. Hey, guys—"

The phone disconnected. Bowman hadn't wanted Silas to end the call, but maybe that was best to focus on getting out safely.

Bowman clenched his teeth so hard they ground together as he stared out the window of the taxi, tapping the phone to his chin. He caught Silas in time, he assured himself. The kid would get out of there safely.

If not, Bowman was to blame. He'd wanted that development so badly that he'd played the devil in Harry's ear. He'd never told Harry to hurt his brother but had elaborated on how Harry would be richer when his poor, suffering brother was laid to rest. Bowman had made most of his fortune by playing people against each other or incentivizing them to follow their own desires, morals aside.

He hadn't told Harry to burn down the theater, but he'd noted that if the old building burned to the ground, there would be nothing left to declare it historical.

If anything happened to Silas or any of the theater staff, Bowman had his own deviousness to blame.

DESPITE LANCE'S IMPECCABLE HOSPITALITY, Phoenix still felt like an imposition. She found she was an impatient patient. The show went on without her while she was confined to the apartment and walks around the block until she completed her course of antibiotics.

Pauline kept her company when Lance left for work or groceries or to run errands. They played chess as his grandmother regaled her with stories of Lance's childhood growing up in Danbury and her own paranormal encounters over the years.

On the third night of her confinement, Phoenix convinced Pauline to let her go to the theater. Lance was working, but it was a Monday, which meant there was no show. The crew had the day off, though some might be lingering to work on costumes or the set.

"I thought I'd find you here," Phoenix said, admiring Lance as he intently worked at his desk.

"Phoenix." With a delighted smile, he stood, removing his reading glasses. "How are you feeling?" He came around the desk to embrace her.

She melted into him. "Better. Stronger."

"You could've called. I would've come home, love."

The rumble of his soft, deep voice against her chest soothed her.

He pulled away to look down at her, keeping his hands on her arms and their bodies close. She'd been living in his home for a few days, but Pauline's presence was like a chaperone, ensuring her interactions with Lance were mostly platonic.

"You scared me when I had to rush you to the hospital."

She looked into his eyes, searching and finding a deep affection laced with a hint of desire. "I'm glad you found me."

"I did find you. After all these years. Now, I'm never letting you go."

Heat bloomed through her core, up her neck, and into her cheeks. "Shouldn't we have a first date before you say something like that?"

He wriggled closer, obviously detecting her attraction to him. "I've danced with you, performed with you, had conversations about our families, and held you in my arms desperate not to lose you. We will take that first date, but I already know what my heart wants." His mouth, gentle yet confident, closed over hers.

She surrendered to the moment, touching and tasting him as she savored the feel of him pressed against her. The kiss was every bit as delicious as she'd dreamed.

A shrill mechanical alarm shattered the blissful movement.

"The fire alarm?" Lance's embrace tightened around her.

Phoenix cringed at the sound. "Who else is here?"

"Carrie, Ray, and Silas—they were working on props."

Hand in hand, they left the back office and headed down the hallway toward the stage. They needed to see that the others reached safety.

Pungent smoke layered along the ceiling and grew denser. They both began coughing.

"Back, back," Lance urged. "We can't go that way. I think it's coming from the costume room."

Flames licked from under the door as the paint bubbled and crackled on the walls.

They doubled back, passing the director's office. Phoenix kept her grip firmly on Lance.

"Rear exit," he said.

"Good thinking."

They would circle around to the rear exit. Hopefully, the others already went out the front. If not... Phoenix shuddered and closed her thoughts to the dismal possibility.

But before they reached it, the smoke grew thick again as the halls radiated heat.

"The fire must be in the props room and wrapped

around to seal us off." Phoenix could hear the roar of flames —just on the other side of the wall like a hungry, angry animal tearing through its cage.

"We'll have to cover our nose and mouth and make a run for it," Lance said.

The lights flickered out, plunging them into darkness. Phoenix's heart ratcheted up, pounding against her ribcage as thick smoke sent her into a coughing fit.

Ten

When the cab stopped, Bowman took in the scene. Smoke billowed out of the top windows of The Magnolia as they glowed a menacing orange. The front doors were propped open and a half dozen firefighters scurried around two engines, bathing the scene in red and white strobe lights.

The cab driver swore as he gaped at the building. Bowman tossed cash at him and ran toward the theater, calling Silas on his phone as he did.

"Mr. B?" His voice sounded strained.

"Silas, where are you?"

"I'm trapped. Oh, man, I think my leg is broken."

"Where?"

"The pit. I fell when the theater went dark."

The orchestral pit, Bowman knew, was in front of the stage before the theater audience seating.

He skirted a parked police cruiser, dashed around a pair of firefighters lugging a hose, and bolted into the burning building, ignoring the shouts and protests erupting behind him.

He flicked on his phone light as he ran down the aisle. The smoke forced him to hunch, then crawl. Fire devoured the rear stage wall, both curtain and wood paneling, while the orange and red flames danced as if performing for an audience.

"Silas!"

"Mr. B!"

"Silas?"

"Down here!"

Bowman reached the orchestra pit—a four-foot drop between the stage and the seats—and peered down. While grimacing in agony, Silas attempted to pull himself to stand.

"Grab on!" Bowman commanded. He wrapped his arms around Silas's torso as the kid clung to his tuxedo jacket and cried out in pain.

He hoisted Silas out and into the aisle between rows of seats. Sweat beaded on his forehead and dripped into his eyes, but there was no time to rest.

"We have to move, Silas. Can you crawl?"

"I can crawl," he said on a wheezy exhale.

Bowman assessed the thickening smoke and encroaching fire as Silas began crawling. He was moving much too slowly.

Bowman shoved to his feet and hoisted Silas over his shoulder. The kid screamed again in agony, but there simply was no other way. Bowman ran down the aisle as fast as he could with the extra weight while he coughed and gagged on the smoke.

When he reached the front doors, a first responder

lifted Silas off of Bowman's shoulder as firefighters dressed in fire-retardant clothing and wearing tanks stormed past him, hoses at the ready to beat back the fiery dragon.

Bowman collapsed to his knees, lungs burning as he gasped for air as a medic came to his rescue.

~

WE'RE HOPELESSLY SURROUNDED, Phoenix thought.

Lance's suggestion to make a run for it through smoke and fire didn't seem like a viable plan.

Singing—harsh and commanding—caught her attention.

The chamber!

"This way." She tugged Lance toward the closet as he turned on the flashlight on his mobile phone. "The chamber. It was used during prohibition for smuggling. There are tunnels."

In the closet, he yanked open the door and ushered her onto the steps that led down to the underground expanse as a wave of fire and smoke cascaded down the hall. He slipped his phone in his pocket in order to pull the door shut with both hands. It sealed, plunging them into darkness.

With a ferocious bellow as if infuriated its victims had escaped, the fire ate into the door, causing what sounded like the collapse of the whole of the storage room ceiling.

The rumbling blast sent Phoenix reeling backward, but strong arms caught her.

"I've got you," Lance said. After steadying her upright, he withdrew his phone again. Light from it illuminated the room.

They scurried down the stairs where clean, moist air replaced the acrid, searing smoke. When they reached the center chamber, Lance paused, checking his phone.

"Poor cell service. I'll try to get through, but it may take the fire department a while to dig us out of here. It sounded as if the entire theater collapsed in on itself—not surprising since it's made of old, flammable wood and decorative tapestries. We could be pinned down here awhile." He raised her hand and kissed the back of it, a gesture she found reassuring. "Good thing it's all stone."

"Do you hear the music?" she asked.

"No."

"It's further away." She pulled out her phone, set the light on, and followed the voice. She'd only ever visited the chamber, singing with Gaston, and never explored the shadows beyond the light.

Lance stayed beside her, still holding her hand. "What's he singing?"

She smiled. "All I Ask of You."

LANCE WALKED HAND-IN-HAND WITH PHOENIX, relieved they'd survived the fire and amazed they were following the voice of a ghost to safety. He'd certainly taken more than one leap of faith in the last few days.

And what would a life with a medium be like? Never dull, certainly. Nana had had a happy marriage for decades despite her eccentricities of having ghosts warn her of impending events.

Did Phoenix want a life with someone who didn't have

any paranormal gifts? He hoped so. He looked forward to dating her and exploring their compatibility.

"All this time," Phoenix began, "Gaston was singing of danger to the theater. Not me."

"Both, I think. And we're alive because he revealed this place to you."

She sucked in a breath and blinked, shielding her eyes as though startled by something bright.

"What's wrong?" Lance asked.

"Gaston. He's singing *So Long, Farewell.*"

Lance thought of the lyrics to *The Sound of Music* song and how they seemed fitting—to say goodbye after a sigh, to be glad to go with a tone of relief. He had Julia, after all, waiting for him.

When Phoenix lowered her chin to her chest, Lance asked, "The ghost is gone?"

"I think he found peace and moved on," Phoenix said. "But '*he lives on within the souls of those who chose to listen to the music of the night.*'"

"Ah. More *Phantom* quotes. Okay. Your phantom saved our lives, and '*he had a heart that could have held the empire of the entire world.*'"

She raised herself up and gave Lance a quick kiss on the cheek. "I'm grateful to have had both of you looking out for me and the theater. Oh! The poor theater. It must be in ruins by now."

When they resumed walking, sunlight revealed a short flight of stairs leading from the tunnel to a gate.

"Ah! There you are!" Nana called to them. "Took your time, didn't you?" She stood, holding a pair of bolt cutters as she swung the iron gate open, rusty hinges squeaking in protest.

"Nana, you never cease to amaze me." Lance grinned.

Phoenix hugged the woman. "Thank you, Pauline." She turned to Lance. "Shall we go see what the theater looks like?"

His smile faded. "I'm afraid so."

~

SIX MONTHS LATER

PHOENIX SANG the last soulful note as Maria in *West Side Story*. She could easily draw pain into her voice—she only needed to think about how it would feel to lose Lance the way Maria lost Tony, the way Charles had lost Julia. But hope resonated in those notes as well, like how Gaston's music had saved her and Lance. The phantom had brought them together and then showed them the way to escape the fire.

They'd finally had that first date after Pauline went back home to England and Phoenix went back to her own apartment. Dinner for two had been romantic and had quickly become a pleasant nightly ritual.

Now, when the lights dimmed on stage, Phoenix stood and turned toward the audience—a packed audience for the first performance at The Magnolia since the fire, which had had its share of local and national headlines.

Donated funds matched by a well-known developer in the community had been used to renovate the theater. She'd glimpsed Mr. Bowman in the crowd tonight seated with his wife. Cillian had introduced him to Phoenix before the show, and Lance had ensured the man had a season pass.

The builders had reused every scrap of wood, unburned theater seat, and salvageable fixture like lights and knobs. The finished product was like a breathtakingly restored antique. A less flammable one.

Cillian's brother had been arrested for the arson, and had shockingly confessed to the murder of the last stage director as well.

Bright lights flooded the stage, and all the performers poured onto it. The audience began to applaud as row after row stood. Phoenix smiled, taking her bow with Ray on one side and Carrie on the other.

Lance approached her, carrying a dozen red roses. When he held them out, she took them, eyes glistening.

"You were magnificent." He leaned closer to be heard over the clapping. "I love you."

He drew back, bent, and kissed her hand.

"I love you, too," she said.

"When we're back at my place tonight, I'll show you just how much."

Anticipation skittered down her spine and settled as heat in her lower abdomen. She looked forward to what he planned to show her.

Life in show biz was never dull, least of all with a man like Lance.

After he led her off stage, she set the roses down and leapt into his arms. She glimpsed the surprised delight in his expression before pressing her lips to his and closing her eyes. Her world burst with light, like fireworks, as their bodies molded together and their mouths collided in passion and desire.

When the kiss ended, he gazed at her as if she was his most prized possession. "*'I have tasted all the happiness the world can offer.'*"

She smiled at his *Phantom of the Opera* quote. "Mmm. That was only the appetizer. We're not done tasting."

She no longer felt the phantom's music guiding her— only her own heart.

Brief Author Note

***** QUICK NOTE FROM THE AUTHOR *****

READY FOR ANOTHER sweet and magical romantic suspense? There are so many delights to enjoy! Keep scrolling for the first chapter in the next book.

IN BOXED SETS

INDIVIDUAL BOOKS
Romancing the Spirit Series #1

Sadie's Spirit / Willow's Windfall
Cassie's Chase / Phoebe's Pharaoh
Vanessa's Valentine / Autumn's Angel
Romancing the Spirit Series #2
Carol's Christmas / Allison's Alibi
Gracelynn's Genie / Michelle's Miracle
Heather's Hero / Chloe's Cupid
Romancing the Spirit Series #3
Sabrina's Storm / Jenny's Justice
Stella's Star / Gigi's Gift
Phoenix's Phantom / Fiona's Freedom

THE CHRISTMAS COLLECTION

Dear Reader

If you enjoyed this book and want to know about future releases by CB Samet you can CLICK HERE to sign up for my mailing list! I promise I won't spam you. I only send an email when I have a new book released, giveaways, or special discounts. And I'll never sell your information. You can also unsubscribe at any time.

Also, as an independent author, I rely heavily on readers to spread the word about books they've read. If you enjoyed this story, kindly let others know by posing a brief comment on social media or leave a review where you purchased it.

Thank you for reading,
CB Samet
www.cbsamet.com

Other Books by CB Samet

Looking for more romantic suspense with more action and sizzle? How about with an urban fantasy twist? Check out my supernatural adventures...

The Shadow Guardians Trilogy

Urban fantasy Norse Mythology Adventure

Get *Raven's Flight, a prequel novella* for FREE. In my newsletter, you'll learn about me, special discounts, and new releases.

Raven's Flight, prequel novella

Raine Down, Book 1

Rosalyn's Run, novella

Storm Surge, Book 2

Anka's Orb, novella

Sky Fall, Book 3

Olympian Awakenings Trilogy

Urban fantasy Greek Mythology Adventure

Grab the prequel exclusively HERE.

Stone Hearts

Winds of Destiny

Flame and Shadow

~

The Rider Files

Romantic Suspense Thrillers

Meridian File / Masters File / Box Set 1

McMillan File / Maltisse File / Box Set 2

Storm File / Sullivan File / Box Set 3

Sharp File / Sizani File / Box Set 4

Rivera File / Rucker File / Box Set 5

Richmond File / Redwood File / Box Set 6

Atlas File / Angel File / Box Set 7

Buy 4book box sets direct from author and save 10%

Payhip. Use code E152M0GZG4

~

The Dr. Whyte Adventure Novels

Thriller Series

Black Gold

Whyte Knight

Gray Horizon

~

Love action/adventure and strong female leads in a fantasy world? Check out my other genre:

The Avant Champion Fantasy Series

The Avant Champion: Rising

Malakai: An Avant Champion Origin of Malos Story (prequel)

The Avant Champion: Honor

The Avant Champion: Ashes

Brothers' Bond: An Avant Champion Malakai Story

The Avant Champion: Conquest

Isabel: An Avant Champion novelette

The Avant Champion: Redeem

Fiona's Freedom

Fiona Stanković came to the US to teach ballet, but hard times have her taking odd jobs and hoping to be able to renew her visa. An offer from a CEO billionaire to teach his younger sister might be the key to financial survival, unless a stalker from her past unravels everything.

Under pressure to marry to keep control of the family business, workaholic Jared Drake sees opportunity in his sister's dance instructor. But he soon discovers his willingness to put his heart and his life on the line to save her.

Sample Chapter

"An arranged marriage?" Jared practically choked on his spiced tea at the breakfast table. He put his electronic tablet in sleep mode so he could stare incredulously at his mother.

She stood by the dining room window wearing a peach

chevron knit dress. Her blonde hair framed her face in big, soft curls. "You're going to lose your inheritance otherwise. What about the Byrne girl?"

"*Woman*, Mother," he corrected, a hint of irritability in his tone. "You can't call a thirty-year-old a girl."

"Well how young is too old? Gwen Stefani was twenty-six when she sang *I'm Just a Girl*."

Jared shook his head. The random facts his mother could summon as a ghost were mind boggling. He was certain she'd never listened to a Gwen Stefani song in her life when she'd been a physical living being.

Obviously sensing she hadn't won the debate, his mother continued, "There are over a thousand adult fiction books with 'girl' in the title and two-thirds of them are actually about women. Eighty percent of them were written by women."

He blinked at her. "I'm sure that's a marketing ploy rather than legitimate examples of calling women 'girls.'"

"Anyway." She waved a hand. "The Byrne *woman's* grandfather has old money and prestige. He owns theaters in New York and restaurants across the country."

His mother's youthful face contrasted the more gaunt-looking one she'd had before she died. One day, she would move on, and Jared would always envision this vibrant version when he thought of her. He often reminded himself how precious the gift the extra time was, though being appreciative proved challenging during moments when she was badgering him about areas of his life she thought were lacking.

"Or, you could marry the Gaines' daughter—though that Missy would be a wild one to pin down."

Appetite soured, Jared pushed his breakfast plate away and rubbed his temples as his mother prattled on, listing other names of eligible women. He had twenty hours of work to cram into a twelve-hour work schedule today, and his mother was trying to set him up with a woman even from beyond the grave.

"What about love?" he asked, plucking his lucky baseball out of his briefcase and tossing it back and forth in his hands.

But even he heard the absurdity of his question. He believed in love, but relationships took time to cultivate. Time was a commodity he didn't have. He didn't need to look at his mother to know she was delivering her famous arched eyebrow look of incredulity.

Stefan entered and made a beeline for Jared's plate.

"Mother is pestering me about an arranged marriage, Stefan. Perhaps you can talk some sense into her."

The lanky butler bristled as he held the plate to cart away. "Lady Drake was a formidable woman in life and equally formidable in death. I have no intention of incurring the wrath of a ghost."

Jared's mother's form flickered by the window as she gave the slightest smirk Stefan couldn't see. Unlike Jared, Stefan couldn't see Laura's ghost, but he could sense her presence and hear her. Jared came from a long line of mediums, though usually they only saw their own deceased family members—probably because they were all workaholics who didn't get out much. Due to their eccentricities, they tried to hire only house staff who were also acquainted with the paranormal.

Stefan was in his sixties and had served Jared's father

before him. He wore a three-piece suit and white shirt every day of his life and lived with a few other staff at the guest house on the property. His long face held a wide mouth and deep-set eyes.

"Will you be needing anything else, sir?"

"No. Sadly, I've lost my appetite." Jared glanced pointedly at his mother who continued to stare out of the window without acknowledging his barb.

As he stood, he placed his napkin on the table and picked up his electronic tablet which had all of his meeting notes for the day. He dropped his baseball back in his briefcase.

Marriage.

He didn't have time for a wife. But he needed one. If he didn't marry, the trust funds would be bequeathed to Jared's younger cousin, who was married, would swoop in to seize the company business. And Douglas Drake, Jared's father's brother's son, had already demonstrated his propensity to spend more than he made without regard for the company's interest. Whereas Jared would use the funds to grow the business and its employees.

"And you have Morgan to look after," his mother added, as if he didn't already know his obligation to his younger sister. "Where is she anyway?"

Jared shook his head. Mother, in her spectral form, could just as easily zip from room to room and find her or use her literal sixth sense, but she obviously wanted to demonstrate her frustration by asking Jared where she was.

"Probably dancing."

"Oh. I wish she would choose something more practical."

Jared tucked his tablet under his arm and took a last sip of his lukewarm tea. "She's only sixteen."

"College in two years."

"Pestering her as a ghost isn't helping."

"Neither is coddling her." With another shake of his head, Jared left the room.

Arranged marriage? The words clinked around inside his head like ice in a dry glass.

How could he entertain the idea of an arranged marriage as his mother had suggested in this modern era? Even if he did, how did one go about arranging it?

Fiona slipped on her thick rubber gloves as she knelt to scrub the bathroom.

"Why are you smiling?" Rhianna asked her. Her brown curls were stuffed under a yellow bandana as she set down a tray of cleaning supplies.

"I have a job tryout this afternoon."

Rhianna doused the mirror in window cleaner and began wiping. "Try out? Like an interview?"

"Interview, yes."

"That's cool. For that ballet thing you do?"

"Yes." That ballet thing she *used* to do, Fiona thought.

She'd come to the US on a work visa specifically to teach ballet, but six months after she moved to Atlanta the studio went under. She hadn't even received her last month's check. Soon, she would need to apply to renew the visa for another year, but she needed to show employment in the field of work she was supposed to be in, not the one she was forced to do to put meat on the table and a roof over her head. '

The roof, she lamented, was a tiny studio apartment the size of a laptop. Used to dancing on an open stage, she felt stifled back and forth between her apartment and cleaning small, grimy spaces.

"So, are you going to quit this job if you get the ballet gig?" Rhianna snorted. "That was a stupid question. Of course, you are."

"No, I can't. This is just teaching a young woman. One on one. It won't be enough money." But maybe if she started with one person—one family—and then earned more, she could not only sustain herself, but she would be an entrepreneur and not at the mercy of someone else's business.

"You know what you should do? Take that luscious Serbian accent and make money on the phone. Lot of lonely men would pay to hear you talk to them." Rhianna laughed.

Fiona let out a humorless chuckle as she scrubbed the grout. She had absolutely no intention of such a thing. She'd taken on ballet at a young age to escape the untrained employment options for the unmarried: laborer or prostitute. And she'd vowed the first time she'd been propositioned would be the last.

She would rather scrub toilets than let a man profit off her body.

~

Fiona tried not to gape at the majestic mansion as she approached the steps to the ornate French doors. Steep roofing of steel gray shingles accentuated the light gray stone masonry and the triple inlet windows.

The house was three stories tall and must have had five fireplaces judging by the smoke stacks. Or perhaps twice as many if they connected to a fireplace on the floor above them. She could only glimpse a few flowers in full spring bloom in the garden winding behind the large, impressive house.

And the house had windows. So many windows. The owner must have employed an army just to clean all of those windows. And many toilets, no doubt. But Fiona wasn't here to scrub anything.

This was her first teaching job since the studio went bankrupt. This was the job she needed to begin a cascade of employment to keep her visa justified. Someone lived in this house whose life was nothing like hers. Someone she would have to impress.

She raised her head higher as she walked down the cobbled driveway and around the circle to the front door. Today was a new beginning for her, and as many of those as she'd had, she'd learned to face them head on.

Before she had a chance to knock, the large, wooden door swung open.

"Stefan!" she cried at the sight of the man greeting her at the door.

"Darling, Fiona. Don't you look lovely." He had soft eyes haloed in wrinkles and gray hair that had gradually thinned over the years. His smile was part of every childhood memory she cherished.

Fiona's heart lit with excitement to see him and gratitude that he'd helped her get this job. She'd been so busy with work that she hadn't seen him since she traveled to the America. Stepping her uncle's arms, she hugged him. His embrace felt a little stiff, making her wonder if the owner of the monstrosity before her discouraged employees from displays of affection.

"How are you?" Stefan backed away and smoothed a hand down his lapel.

"Wonderful. Thank you for this opportunity."

Tryouts.

Except, instead of trying out for the role of ballet performer, she was trying out for the role of teacher. Her nervousness seemed equally intense, as if she was doing the former with her future hanging in the balance.

"It would be wonderful to have you working here. I'm sure you'll get the job. But look at you. So thin. America has not been kind." He gestured for her to come inside the mansion.

"Kinder than life would have been staying in Serbia."

"*Naravno*," he said, *of course*, softly with a slight bow of his head, a gesture she thought perhaps he did many times per day as a sign of humble subservience.

Fiona walked through the house, speechless at the site of the long hallways, enormous rooms, high vaulted ceilings and space. So much space. Stefan waxed poetically about the various rooms and their expensive art or what celebrity had been inside them over the decades.

Fiona marveled at the open expanse of it all. She could dance through the hallways from room to room without risking touching anything or tripping over anyone's junk piles. There was no clutter. And no dust. The house could almost be a museum except for the ambience of a home. Warm colors emanated from the furniture, walls, paintings, and curtains creating a welcoming environment.

They reached the ballroom, an endless open floor of light and dark patterns of wood. A girl sat in an out of place bean bag chair next to a stand with a pitcher of water as she surfed on her phone. Brown hair streaked with bold gold highlights was twisted into braids on either side of her head. She wore leggings and a loose-fitting top along with dance shoes.

"Morgan, this is Fiona, your new dance instructor," Stefan said.

Morgan nodded but didn't look up from her phone as she finished texting someone. After she pressed the SEND button, she stood up and gave Fiona an appraising look.

Fiona squared her shoulders. Fiona straightened her spine. She'd earned her place on stages across Europe. She could handle one teenage girl.

Time to make an amazing first impression.

This wasn't just a job. It was a lifeline—maybe her last one.

<<< KEEP READING >>>